LE TÉLÉPHONE

Other books by
Henry May

Rough Cut
Smugglers
The Long Village
Catch Up
The Tidnor Wood Story
Woolfox Lodge
Semilong
Penmeath
The Roaches

LE TÉLÉPHONE

Henry May

Matador
9 Priory Business Park,
Wistow Road, Kibworth Beauchamp,
Leicestershire, LE8 0RX
Tel: 0116 279 2299
Email: books@troubador.co.uk
Web: www.troubador.co.uk/matador
Twitter: @matadorbooks

ISBN 978 1789018 448

British Library Cataloguing in Publication Data.
A catalogue record for this book is available from the British Library.

Typeset in 11pt Aldine by Troubador Publishing Ltd, Leicester, UK

Matador is an imprint of Troubador Publishing Ltd

To Natalie, Alison and John.
"A chance encounter blossomed into a beautiful friendship."

CHAPTER ONE

Perhaps I owed the Ten Commandments for the story that I am about to relate. Well, not actually THE Ten Commandments but rather a cider apple bearing that name.

I was staring up at a tree laden with rosy red apples in my newly acquired orchard when an old boy sidled up to me. "That be Ten Commandments." I swivelled round ready to chide the interloper for encroaching on my land without an invitation. Noticing in the nick of time that I had left open the gate from the lane, I managed to bite my tongue, so to speak. "But I 'spect you knows that," added my visitor.

A clever piece of countryman's guile hidden in an innocent statement that also served as the question, "Was I knowledgeable on the subject of cider fruit or was I just another townie with enough money to afford a black and white cottage deep in the Herefordshire countryside?" Nevertheless I felt some gratitude that the man was at least talking to me.

"'Erefordshire variety what don't make good cider though. Needs mixing." Looking roundabout he added, "You've got enough varieties 'ere to sort that out."

That was true enough. The orchard had once been home to about fifty trees judging by the stumps and the dead men standing. Thirty-seven were still fertile in fruiting terms but only about twenty prolifically so. All were old, in their dotage, which prompted me to ask cheekily, "are these trees as old as you are?"

1

The stranger's eyes glinted with good humour. "Thereabouts."

"That would be about fifty then?" I suggested, deliberately understating by, I estimated, ten years at least.

The brown weather-beaten face broke into a wry half smile. "If you reckons I be fifty then you'd better git your thinking cap on, mister, or git yerself a pair of spectacles." There was a touch of scorn to be had there no doubt.

"Sixty then?"

"I were seventy-two last Whitsuntide," he revealed nonchalantly. "And I was in short breeches when this ere orchud was planted."

"You remember seeing it planted then?"

"Aye, that I do. Bloke named Potter lived in the 'ouse with his missus. Then came old Arthur Bates. The Palmers and their two daughters were before you came along, but I 'spect you knows that. Least, there were two to start with. Christine got caught with a babby and drowned 'erself in the pond in yon garden."

"What garden?" I asked with rising alarm.

"The one back of your 'ouse?" said the old man mischievously. "Corse they filled it up soon afterwards."

"Then there was the Arkwrights; a couple of real fokkers they was," he said, looking sheepish for engaging in crude language with a total stranger.

"Before or after the Palmers?" I asked proving that I had been attentive.

"Before of course," scowled my visitor as though I should have known.

When I dwelt on this conversation afterwards – and dwell on it I did at length, I came to the realisation that my visitor's main mission, on spying me in the orchard, could have been to spoil my day by acquainting me with one of Well Cottage's ghosts. Bizarrely I had no knowledge of the previous owners, or their tragedy, as I had effectively purchased from the Building Society that had foreclosed on them.

"Missus Palmer took it bad and nagged and nagged her 'ubby to go sort out the young bugger what put Christine up the spout. But Mark Palmer was a bit of a runt, not man enough for the job, and they moved right away. Had no choice I reckon; the way people talk round 'ere."

"O.K., I interrupted." I'd heard enough detrimental about my new home for one day. "Tell me about Ten Commandments? What's your name by the way?"

"Sam Williams."

"I'm Des Harper," I volunteered holding out my hand.

Sam ignored my offer of a handshake keeping both his hands firmly into the pockets of a shabby brown raincoat. He turned back to the tree. "Cut them apples open, crossways, and there be ten red dots spread round the core. Ten dots for ten commandments," he added for good measure. "Don't make good cider on their own but mix 'em with sweet Yarlington Mills' and now you're talking. You've got a couple of Yarlingtons up yonder. I'll show yer if yer want?"

Unbeknown to me at the time, that introduction proved to be the start of a long friendship – or perhaps a better description would be 'acquaintanceship'. I came to be drawn to Sam because of his dry wit, his local knowledge and his practicality with all manner of things to do with the countryside. His interest in me deepened as soon as he discovered that I kept a keg of draught cider in Well Cottage's cellar. I would soon be puzzled to discover that Sam would shy away from descending into the cellar himself, for reasons he never put voice to however hard I pushed for an answer. Instead I would oblige him by bringing up, as required, an old enamel, two quart jug foaming at the brim with his unfiltered yellow liquid.

The season for cider making was nigh and early apple varieties were sprawled generously on the ground. "What should I do with them?" I asked Sam.

"Nowt," replied Sam dismissively. "They're not worth the effort of picking up."

"I was talking to a guy in the Dog and Duck and he says Bulmers buy apples," I queried, referring to the world's largest cider maker and their sprawling factory in the centre of Hereford.

"You'd need a contract to sell to 'em to Bulmers and they buy by the trailer load, tons at a time."

"Not according to this bloke I met. He says that you can take them into the factory in sacks in the boot of a car."

Sam's eyes flickered in surprise that I had discovered a local practice, a concession to locals by the cider maker, without his help. Bulmers may well have been the biggest cider makers in the world but they nevertheless obliged a local custom going back perhaps a century or more, of accepting apples from locals in the smallest of quantities. "Well, yeh, that may be so. But by the time you've picked the buggers up, washed 'em, found clean sacks and delivered them to the mill in 'ereford, what's in it for you? It's not as though you're short of a bob or two by the look of it. Word is that you paid a tidy sum for Well Cottage," he added somewhat sheepishly.

He was right of course. I had taken early retirement from a lucrative career in the City of London and had no need to augment my wealth with the few quid that the fruit would earn. "Making some cider hereabouts would be an interesting diversion surely?" I countered. "Couldn't we make some Sam?" I asked hopefully. My life's work experience depended on the ability to recognise and draw in people with specialist skills.

"We? Not fucking likely," he retorted so quickly as to not allow himself time to ameliorate his language.

That seemed final enough but I was not about to write off the idea completely.

By a very strange coincidence I met another stranger in the Dog and Duck that very night and, the subject being fresh in my mind, I aired my lamentation to the stranger. Being on the third pint of excellent draught bitter I must have become quite passionate about the prospect of producing Well Cottage cider. I should have twigged that one enthusiast was talking to another.

"I know a man who is selling all the equipment you need to make your own cider," said my companion whom, I soon learned, was a car salesman for a big garage on the Worcester Road out of Hereford. "I've seen it and it's the real McCoy."

The fuel inside me ignited my interest no doubt. "It's for sale, you say?" In my mind's eye there in that toasty warm bar of the Dog and Duck the deal was ready to be made.

"Yeh. There's only one small problem though."

My heart sank a little. Why was there ALWAYS a problem to a cinch of an idea? "Which is?"

"My mate what's selling it lives in France."

"And the equipment is?" I suppose that I knew what the answer would be.

"In France."

Another seemingly good idea bit the dust. "It would just have to be."

"But it's only in Normandy, just across the Channel." Salesmen always have a positive take for everything – it's part of their psyche.

"Only," I repeated dismissively.

"It's not that far away. You could catch a ferry from Portsmouth to some place ending in 'stram', in Northern France," argued my tormentor.

"Ouistreham , near Caen," I enlightened him. I had toured the D-Day beaches with Angela one glorious summer many years ago.

"Yeh, something like that. His place is about forty miles from there – in the country – easy to find. Patrick's a real cool dude. He'll give you a good deal."

"Patrick's Irish?"

"So?"

"And he drives a white van with a caravan behind," I responded cynically.

The salesman took a pull on his pint to give himself time to work out my meaning. The penny dropped and he spluttered into a guffaw. "No, no, Patrick's not a diddy. He used to work with me but his wife's a Normande, more nationalistic than Marine Le Penn. She got homesick living over here and poor Pat had no choice other than relocate."

"What's your name? I asked.

"Pete, Peter Brody. And yours?"

"Des, Desmond Harper." We shook hands. It's kind of you Pete," I repeated, "but this isn't going to work."

"Course it'll work, Des. You don't look the jacker sort. Tell you what, I'll give Pat a ring now."

"At this time of night? They're an hour ahead of us in France. Patrick will be in bed, tucked up with his wife."

"Naw, he's an owl. Anyway, even if he is in bed, we salesmen work a twenty-four hour shift when it comes to a deal." With that, before I could protest further, Peter searched in his jacket pocket for his mobile phone, slipped off his stool and made his way outside.

My first thoughts were to do a runner through the pub's side door. Instead I found myself catching the barmaid's eye and silently signing her to pull two more pints. As I waited for Peter I gave some thought to my adversary. He was perhaps the archetypal, slick car salesman type. Fortyish at least, he was built like a rugby forward, solid and tall and soberly dressed in a charcoal black suit, a white shirt and patterned tie. His shoes stood out particularly; black and polished to such a shine almost to the point of being twin mirrors. I would put money that he had a duster in his trouser pocket. His hair was short and thinning, immaculate too, and his face suggested that it had never succumbed to the ministrations of a cheap bag of razors.

I didn't think that there was any chance of my popping off to France – at least not on some wild goose chase – but playing out this form of charade was interesting if not compelling and far better than being thrashed on the pool table by an underage yokel.

Peter took his time and I was halfway down the new pint before he came bouncing back into the bar with a huge grin on his face. "I've smashed this one for you Des," he announced patting my shoulder with a familiarity that suggested that we had known each other since school days. "The gear is in apple pie condition" He stopped to admire his unwitting analogy. A press and a broyeur – that's an apple masher I'm told – just three hundred Euros if you collect. I reckon he'd take two-fifty if you're cute." Peter stopped to read my face but I deliberately gave nothing away. "I didn't know that Pat's wife is now running a B&B. They'll put you up at a discounted rate. What's more, if you go this coming week-end their village fete is on. That's an offer you'd be silly to turn down, Patrick says. And if you take your wife with you there wouldn't be any extra charge. You can't say fairer than that." Peter finished his old pint and, first nodding his thanks, started on the fresh one, all the while watching my facial expression. I found it hard to stay dead pan.

"I don't have a wife," I said slowly after a significant pause. Peter's face showed his frustration recognising the possibility of being led off course.

"Well, take the boyfriend then," he quipped with a grin and a twinkling eye.

I treated the remark with the good humour it deserved. "I did have a wife but sadly she died suddenly three years ago." An image of Angela's smile flashed up accompanied by the usual pang of remorse. "Are you married Peter?" I asked, keen to move the conversation away from myself.

"I've been married twice and divorced twice. The last one took me to the cleaners," he added ruefully. And, reverting back to the business on hand, "Take the lady friend then." He looked me up and down. "You look as though you have plenty of life in you yet, nudge, nudge. You can practise French kissing." He laughed expansively at his own wit.

The manner in which my companion's eyes kept flicking towards the barmaids proud bosom suppressed any sympathy that I might have had for his marital predicament yet I smiled involuntarily, "No lady friend either. Anyway, how would I get the gear back to the U.K.? I only own a small car."

"We do van hire at the garage. I'll give you a week-end for the price of a day. You can't say fairer than that."

As a testament to Peter Brody's skills as a salesman I wobbled back up the lane to Well Cottage a little before midnight according to the clock on the tower of St. Edmund's church, having signed on the dotted line as it were. Capitulated most like. I collapsed into bed too befuddled with real ale to have any doubts – they came tumbling in at me the following morning.

My breakfast was black coffee followed by black coffee. Several times I reached for the telephone and punched in the numbers that Peter Brody had written for me on a beer mat. I just couldn't bring myself to complete the sequence and transmit. Why was that? Pride… and the old fashioned idea that a man's word is his bond? Not only would I disappoint

Peter but he had made the booking for the coming week-end with his mate Patrick. Besides making myself look like an arsehole in their eyes there was undoubtedly an element of wishing to tempt Fate. I was always a sucker for doing that, and still am to be honest. So I did eventually make a telephone call that morning but not to Peter, rather to book a passage with Brittany Ferries for the 0830 boat from Portsmouth that coming Friday.

When Sam called by enterprisingly for what would become his regular tea-time "harn of cider" as he called it (harn being his dialect for 'horn') he gave me dog's abuse. Not so much verbally, he was of the touching the forelock genre, but through facial expressions and body language. "If you've got yer mind set on makin' cider why the eff…, why the hell do you want to make it the French way? Them Froggies don't know how to make proper cider. 'Sides, you can't trust 'em. Look what they done in the war. They scarpered when the going got tough." I gave up. There was no placating the old fart. All I could do was keep the cider flowing until he toddled off home, wheezing and grumbling under his breath.

It turned out that Peter's offer of a week-end for the price of a day was honoured by the humourless manager of the Vehicle Hire Department at Rillington's garage, but that was as far as any discounts carried. "Week-end" translated to Friday evening to first thing on Monday morning. I needed a vehicle, a long wheelbase Transit, from Thursday lunchtime to Tuesday morning. Those extra two days (half days counted as whole days) cost me dear. My attempt to "have a word" about the cost with Peter proved fruitless. According to the Hire Manager he was "not available".

To add insult to injury I had failed to realise initially that I was obliged to book a hotel in Portsmouth for the Thursday night, otherwise I would have needed to rise in the dead of night in order to drive the three hours to Portsmouth on Friday morning. The total price of the press and broyeur had more than doubled before I had set a foot outside of my front door. Still, what the hell, I could afford the cost … what price the experience?

There was a sense of urgency that had been an undercurrent in the decision process. The apples in my orchard were already falling from the trees in significant quantities and, although bruising and some decomposition can improve the quality of the eventual cider, Sam reliably informed me, they wouldn't stay usable forever. If the equipment that I was intending to buy needed minor repairs before it could be utilised then I needed to move quickly.

With some misgivings I gave Sam a set of keys to Well Cottage on the understanding that whilst he checked out the security of my dwelling he restricted himself to no more than four "harns" per visit. For my generosity Sam treated me to an explanation of the history of 'a horn of cider' .In the "good ole days" farmers were expected to provide cider as part of a labourer's wages. At the end of the working day the men would stand in a circle round the cider barrel and pass round the horn – a cow's horn made into a small cup, containing a couple of large swallows. Round and round it would go, each man drinking a full horn and woe betide any man who took too long about quaffing the contents. Of course, Sam's "harn" when visiting me was at least a half pint glass and a larger one if I inadvertently let him choose. Whilst I was away he would just have to summon up courage and venture down the cellar himself.

Thursday came all too soon and when I arrived at the garage to pick up the van, surprise, surprise, Peter was there to greet me, his face cracking into a broad smile. "Of course you can leave your car in our pound, Des, and there'll be no charge for that."

"That's very kind of you," I thanked him sarcastically, "very kind indeed."

CHAPTER TWO

Six and a half hours on the boat was tedious to put it mildly; five and three quarter hours sailing time and the balance spent loading and disembarking. I hadn't thought to book myself into a day cabin until the *Normandie* was clear of the Isle of Wight. Had I done so I would have added to my tally of sleep.

Happily the school holidays had long finished and the ferry was only half full although its vehicle decks were at bursting point with juggernauts. Their drivers, from every country in Europe I imagined, were easily recognisable on the three passenger only decks. The downside was two coach loads of energetic and excitable French schoolchildren making the most of their freedom before having to succumb again to the expectations of their parents. Who could blame them?

I had nipped into the Cider Museum in Hereford on the Wednesday and purchased an elementary book about cider making. Studying its contents accounted for just an hour of my marine entombment. I cannot say that I learned all that much either, but the book served to re-enforce my hitherto shaky knowledge of the process. I had not expected any reference to French equipment and techniques and so on that score I could not claim to be disappointed.

I read that most artisan cider makers claim that the best cider is achieved by using mainly windfalls showing evidence of bruising and some decomposition. But in my short experience of a Herefordshire autumn I had seen acres of commercial apple orchards being shaken by specialist machinery. Huge trailers carry the apples, often twelve tons and more at a time, to the voracious crushing mills at Bulmers and Westons factories and even farther afield. There they are macerated into a rough pulp and then hydraulically pressed to extract the juice which is fermented in huge tanks or vats.

The traditional method of cider making in England, still widely practised by artisans and small cider makers, is to pulp the apples in a hand operated mill sometimes colloquially termed a "scratter". The pulp is then piled onto a square porous sheet called a "hair" (the early hairs were made of horse hair). The corners are then folded in to create a parcel of sorts. The hairs are stacked one upon another in a press to form a "cheese". A parcel-sized wooden board surmounts the cheese which facilitates an equal pressure downwards intent on slowly squeezing out the juice through the means of a hand-operated screw. Thereby apple juice leaks out from the perforations in the hairs, is collected and transferred into a container where the fermentation process will start.

Even modest presses can be large and heavy and I began to worry that Patrick's version would not fit into the Transit van. That would be the final irony having invested considerable time, energy and money in getting to France only to be thwarted because I had not asked the appropriate questions in the first place. "Shit," or, as the French might say, *merde*.

In the main cafeteria at the sharp end of the *Normandie* I spent an hour or so studying a large scale map of Basse Normandy and of the Department of Calvados in particular. I found St. Bartholemu sans Eglise tucked away in a forested area and calculated it to be about an hour's drive from Caen, should I not be held up in traffic.

I was not fazed by having to drive on the right. I had visited Europe a good few times on holidays with Angela and our two children. Once I fixed in my mind the need to keep the pavement, or grass verge, next to my near side, then driving is virtually a piece of cake. The only serious incident I had was in nearly missing the turnoff I needed to access Caen's *périphérique* , or ring road. It was badly signed and I had to make a late swerve to the right which earned me a long, deep throated honk from a Spanish truck that had been sitting hard on my tail for several kilometres beforehand. You would think that us fellow "commercials" would look after each other. I lowered my window preparing to give him the one finger salute – but thought better of it in time. I nearly overlooked the fact that my van had "Rillingtons Van Hire" writ large across its rear doors. That Spanish bastard could probably read that much in English and I could be a marked man from thereon.

Although St. Bartholemu was fairly well tucked away in beautiful wooded countryside I found it with relative ease, as I did the remote Clery residence, some two kilometres from the village. A prominent sign advertised the accommodation as *Chambres d'Hôte*. Nothing so prosaic as "B & B" for Patrick's patriotic wife.

Many times I had been bemused by the crystal public school English spoken by the sons of self-made Scotsmen, their fathers remaining wedded to broad dialects. Hitherto I had not experienced a similar disparity in an Irishman. Nor did Patrick's physical appearance bear any of what I might have regarded as native characteristics. Ramrod tall, athletically muscular, blond and groomed to perfection, the man represented the archetypal English gentleman.

In contrast there could be little doubt that willowy Evette was of the French *classe supériere*. She deigned to shake my hand there being no question of a traditional *Normande* perfunctory kiss on both cheeks. Her slim hand was as limp as the trace of the smile she allowed me, a concession that did not extend to her eyes. If I had been told that Evette was a model whose photographs were in demand for chic Parisian magazines, I would have experienced no element of doubt on that score.

Patrick bade me "dump" my week-end bag in my allotted *chambre*. I had once spent a romantic week-end in the George V Hotel in Paris costing one thousand Euros a night minimum. I could not say that my room in the George V was superior to the bedroom in which I was standing. Beyond my initial astonishment and then admiration, I started to feel grubby and gauche and consequently uneasy about the size of the bill that I would be presented with on Monday morning. I began to wish that I had never met that bloody salesman in the Dog and Duck...

Patrick appeared reluctant to show me the press and apple mill that evening, suggesting that I was too tired after a long day spent travelling and I would have a better disposition in the morning. I was politely insistent. If the equipment was a dog then I would have the perfect excuse to walk away then and there and go find a more economic billet in a nearby town. I was not on the brink of becoming a sexagenarian for nothing. Of course, I was careful not to give my host any clue as to my reasoning.

Patrick reluctantly led the way out to the back of the *manoir* into what had once been a stable yard elegantly bordered on three sides by smart granite buildings. I was led to one corner and into what had once been the tack room judging by the intricate wall brackets that had once served to hang saddles and bridles – now long forgotten. I was then presented with a jumble of wood and metal lying beside what I was now confident in recognising as a free standing cider mill.

I gasped involuntarily, literally lost for words. I caught Patrick watching my reaction intently. "I recognise the scratter but what is that pile of junk next to it?"

"What you call a scratter, dear boy, is called a *broyeur* in France." interjected the Irishman.

"That's as maybe, Patrick, but that heap next to the broyeur or whatever you call the thing, is nothing like anything I've seen in England."

"That's because it is a French press, Desmond," responded Patrick with exaggerated pronunciation mimicking as if he were talking to an idiot. "Didn't Pete Brody make that clear?"

"He most certainly didn't," was my anguished reply.

"He can be a real bugger that bloke," chided Patrick unconvincingly.

"I may look stupid to you but no way am I buying a pile of junk as it stands."

"Of course not," soothed the immaculate Irishman. "You've jumped the gun, Des. Dinner will soon be served in the dining room. Why not spruce yourself up and join our other guests. By morning I will have the press assembled and you can then make a quality judgement. I am sure you will be suitably impressed and will want to grab my hand off at the price I am proposing to charge you. You'll feel guilty for robbing a poor Irishman, so you will."

On that note Patrick and I walked off in different directions.

"We are visiting *Mont Saint-Michel* tomorrow, why don't you come with us Mr. Harper?" invited the Dutch lady sitting opposite. Her husband sitting beside her nodded in silent agreement. "I believe that you have a mini version of the South Cornwall Coast? Near Penzance? I am Dolores and my husband is Elbert." There were four other guests at the table that night; two couples, all French. That made seven white haired people in all, allowing for the men folk who were all in various stages of balding.

We were being served by a mature woman in a discrete maid's uniform whose husband, I was later to learn, was the *chef de cuisine.* The food was excellent, the wines well chosen and the atmosphere convivial despite the fact that the French foursome spoke only a smattering of English and the Dutch pair little French but commendable English. "Madame Laignel speaks English beautifully," confided Dolores, "but she pretends not to when it suits her, and especially when there are Brits within earshot."

"Madame Laignel? I don't believe that I have met her yet," I observed impassively.

"I saw you being introduced to her when you arrived," said Dolores with a look of surprise.

"The only woman that I have met is Patrick's wife."

"That's Madame Laignel. Yes, I know it's confusing. She prefers to keep her maiden name. She's a proud *Normande* you see."

"And she pretends not to speak English," added Elbert, evidently not having heard his wife making the same comment moments earlier.

"Why is that?" I asked feigning interest.

Dolores, blushing slightly said, "Oh, I don't know."

"Yes you do Dol. You just don't want to hurt Mr. Harper's feelings," Elbert interjected.

"Desmond," I protested.

"You see, Desmond," the Dutchman continued, "she dislikes Anglo-Saxons." With a broad smile he added, "Dolores and I think that she is trying to revenge Trafalgar and Waterloo."

"And conveniently ignores D-Day too?" I blurted.

"No, Desmond," Dolores said cautiously," "but on that theatre she concentrates more on the Free French landings on Sword Beach and the deliberately suppressed reports of G.I.'s raping local girls as if doing so was a just reward for their conquest and sacrifices."

"But she's married into the Anglo-Saxon race?" I said, not willing to explore that aspect of the invasion of which I knew nothing.

"Aren't the Irish Celts?" corrected Dolores diplomatically, downgrading her superior knowledge by way of a question.

With dinner completed and all seven guests in various states of gastronomic contentment, the door from the hall opened and in walked the lady herself, attired immaculately in an evening dress that allowed her to glide over to her French guests whilst allowing me and the Dutch couple the briefest of acknowledgements in the process. When seated she entered into animated conversation with her compatriots. I saw this as a suitable opportunity to retire to my bed chamber after accepting the offer of a trip to the famous *Mont Saint-Michel* the following morning.

I slept as soundly as I should have done after an exhausting day and excellent dinner.

Breakfast was essentially coffee and croissants, jam and baguettes. That was more than sufficient as much of the previous evening's meal seemed to be queuing in my stomach awaiting processing. I was alone in the dining room, admiring an antique Vienna clock, ticking rhythmically on the back wall, when Patrick strolled in.

"Morning Des," he greeted brightly. "I trust that you slept well?" I would have affirmed had he paused to await my reply. "Dolores has told me that you are off to the Mont with them today."

I nodded, my mouth full of buttery croissant and strawberry jam.

"You do that and by the time you return I'll have the press up and running. Have a nice day." Like a genie he was gone as quickly as he had appeared.

Mont Saint-Michel, is a World Heritage Site and one of the most visited tourist attractions in France, only Parisian monuments scoring higher. Despite being Autumn and outside the prime tourist season, the location was crawling with humanity; literally shoulder to shoulder in the cobbled, medieval street that led steeply upwards to the Abbey sitting atop the granite pile. Dolores ran out of puff – or so she said – and declined to make the steep climb to the abbey. Elbert muttered darkly to himself; questioning her motives no doubt. Nevertheless as the day was warm and sunny, he and I were content to sit and chat outside several small bars cum restaurants whilst Dolores went off patronising the seemingly endless curio shops and boutiques. Consequently we were never to make it up to the famous abbey that day; mammon won out, hands down.

A simple but excellent *plat du jour* in a small auberge on the return journey rounded off a pleasant excursion, one that I was glad not to have missed. That late afternoon, back at our *chambres d'hôtes*, my newly promoted Dutch friends retired for a siesta whilst I, with mounting trepidation, searched out Patrick.

I found him rubbing linseed oil into a contraption which I didn't immediately recognise as a cider press as it bore no resemblance to its English cousin. A heavy, legged, square base, from the centre of which rose a thick metal rod to the height of about six feet. The top twelve or so inches of the rod had been manufactured in the form of a screw. Standing on the base, edge to edge, was a circular frame, perhaps two feet six inches high, consisting of a series of vertical slats, maybe numbering fifty or thereabouts. The gap between each slat was small. I would later realise that this slatted frame was in two halves each held together by three peripheral iron bands which, locked together, made a perfect and rigid circle. Beside the contraption lay a pile of heavy wooden blocks and other shapes and some business-like, heavy metal objects too.

"The apples go into the basket," Patrick explained. "When it's full these two plates are placed over the top of them," he said, selecting two heavy, wooden half circles from out of the pile on the floor. "They form a circular plate to which downward pressure can be efficiently exerted. These heavy wooden blocks strategically placed on the circular plate act as spacers. This heavy metal ratchet thingy is screwed into the central rod and creates downward pressure to compress the milled apples and hey presto – out squeezes the juice."

"The juice is squeezed out through these upright wooden slats?" I asked dubiously.

"Yep. it trickles down to the base platform where it is funnelled into a bucket or whatever. I am afraid that you will have to provide your own bucket."

I walked up to the press and to the apple mill standing close by, giving them, what I would like to have classed to be, a thorough inspection. Patrick stood to one side patiently. I wondered what old Sam Williams would make of all this. Although as different as chalk and cheese from its English counterpart, the press seemed much easier for an amateur to operate and certainly more user friendly when it came to transportation and storage. I scratched my head and pulled on the lobe of my right ear.

"O.K., Patrick, I am interested, depending on the price. What do you want for it?"

The man pretended to take some thinking time. "Well, because you're a good friend of Peter – and have come all this way at some expense – I'll knock it down to eight hundred Euros."

"Eight hundred Euros?" I squealed. "Eight fucking hundred Euros. That bloody mate of yours told me that the starting price would be three hundred Euros."

Patrick affected a laugh of astonishment. "That's Pete for you. No conscience. I think that he's fed you one."

19

"One what?"

"A whopper. He's known for it."

However much I twisted and turned, however many faults I could find with the state of the equipment, even down to a few woodworm holes, Patrick remained impassive and immovable. At least I thought so until he suddenly conceded, "I'll tell you what, Desmond. You've come a long way and I'd hate to see you go back empty handed. I'll knock fifty Euros off the price of the press and only charge you for two nights for your accommodation instead of three."

"That's very decent of you, Patrick," I replied with undisguised sarcasm, knowing full well that he had me by the bollocks. I had been stupid enough not to have negotiated the price of my accommodation before being handed the bedroom key and anything supposedly "knocked off" could so easily be "added on". Full board at an upmarket *chambre d'hôte* could easily be a hundred Euros a night if not more, much more. The best that I could possibly achieve would be 'damage limitation'.

"I'll tell you what I'll do, Patrick. Eight hundred Euros all in?"

"All in? Accommodation included?" Patrick mimed shock.

"Yep, accommodation included. Take it or leave it. No deal, and I'll pack my bags right now and head up to Calais. I can exchange my ticket for the next sailing, no sweat. I'll pay you for just one night and you'll lose out big time."

"Cash?"

"Of course," I replied hoping my reserves stretched that far and amazed by my host's apparent climb down.

Patrick gave me a wry smile. "Nice one Des. Nine hundred Euros all in and it's a deal. Has to be cash though."

We shook hands. I knew that I had been stuffed but as a chicken rather than a turkey – that was some consolation.

"Come with me and I'll show you something that might interest you Des," said Patrick leading me out of the stable into the yard. He opened one of the other stable doors and ushered me inside. The place was stuffed with antiques and bygones of every description imaginable. Silently I was led to a second stable and then a third with the same result. I voiced my surprise and approval.

"A second string to my bow, Des, or a third or fourth," he added as an afterthought." I go to what you would call car boot sales. They're called *vide greniers* here, translates as empty attics, not quite the same thing as car boot sales. My business is to buy from them and encourage dealers come here and buy from my stock. And they do, from the U.K. mainly but also Holland and Germany, and usually they go back with their vans full to bursting."

"I'm impressed."

"As it so happens it's the turn of St. Bartholemu sans Eglise tomorrow; their annual *vide grenier*. Would you care to accompany me?"

"Not half," I breathed enthusiastically.

"Means getting up at sparrow fart. Early worm and all that."

"No problem. Count me in."

At dinner that night the four French guests tried to join us in friendly conversation but the language barriers proved insuperable and we were all glad to return to the status of the previous evening. Madame Laignel, again stunningly attired, rewarded me and my Dutch friends a brief nod before settling into energetic conservation with her French guests. Dolores gave me a wan smile as we three carried on as before.

Patrick knocked my door at six o'clock in the morning and I descended soon after to find a tray awaiting me with a pot of coffee and a brace of croissants. No sooner had I gulped and gobbled than I was bundled into Patrick's big Renault van and we were off down the lane.

At a crossroads on the outskirts of the village the road ahead was obstructed by an improvised barrier consisting of a diversion sign pointing to the left. Patrick ignored this and inched the van round the impediment. Seeing the quizzical look on my face he explained, "You'll not see the likes of this in England. The village is in purdah for much of the day for reasons you are about to discover." A short distance further on I could see that the road was again barred but on this occasion with stalls and suchlike, some in the process of being set up whilst others were already laid out with wares. A few potential buyers were evident even at that early hour. Patrick pulled over and parked in a manner which in England what would be adjudged as illegal. "Damn, I've already got competition. I'm going to have to leave you." With that he jumped out of the van and fairly galloped towards the action ahead. There did not seem to be any problem with leaving the van unlocked so I shrugged and set of alone in the same direction.

My first *vide grenier* was a source of amazement. The whole of the main road through the village was in the process of becoming awash with improvised tables and trestles, or just piles of stuff, on both sides of the highway. There was spillage too into side streets, whilst another set had taken occupancy of the Marie's car park. A good number of sellers were semi-professional, making a business out of their selling. But most were local people from St. Bartholemu and villages thereabouts, many pitches manned by whole families, from Grandma down to sleeping babies. There were even some stalls right outside people's houses, their front doors wide open offering the curious the bonus of an intriguing glimpse inside.

The village hall was thrown open to offer its toilet facilities whilst the main hall was set up as a rudimentary bar, selling wee cups of black coffee at a Euro a throw. I was surprised to see that a number of patrons were sitting with small tumblers of red wine. Red wine for breakfast? Strange breed these French. Outside were long trestles with rickety bench seats and all the paraphernalia to cook *saucisses et frites* over charcoal. As the day wore on, it being sunny and warm, this amateur outfit was undoubtedly set to do a roaring trade.

Although there were more than enough stalls and pitches to grab my attention along the main street, for some inexplicable reason I diverted into a side road where there were fewer than a dozen sellers. Whilst more buyers were in evidence along the main thoroughfare as the sun rose higher in the sky, the street that I had arbitrarily favoured was being largely ignored. At the far end I was confronted by a dilapidated decorator's paste table with very few items on display. The centrepiece was an old telephone which caught my attention and seemed to beckon me over.

I did not know the first thing about old telephones and especially not French ones. This one was all black and a mixture of iron and Bakelite. I would have said "1930's" but I really had no idea. Its shape was the old fashioned pillar type with a cradle on top in which rested the handset. There was also a separate and matching 'listening' earpiece. I had seen modern copies made of plastic disguised as onyx in high street showrooms. The cord from the circular base to the handset and ear piece looked complete and somehow shabbily added to the instrument's provenance. The cord, which would have connected to the telephone exchange, was missing.

I moved forward and took the item in my hand on the pretext of examining it more carefully whereas in fact I was drawing up courage to enquire in French as to its price on one hand and also to try and work out the item's worth to me. Behind the stall stood a couple, pensioners, perhaps in their seventies or otherwise having had a hard life. "French peasants" came cruelly to mind, but they did look shabby, care-worn and short of a Euro or two. *"Combien, s'il vous plait?"*

I was interrogating the man but the woman spoke after the two of them had exchanged glances. 'Knowing glances' I would come to say in retrospect. *"Soixante Euros"*. Sixty Euros, they seemed to have agreed.

"Trente," I countered. Thirty Euros.

They looked at each other hard and long and the eventual consensus between them was a surprising *"Oui Monsieur."*

If I knew then what I know now I would have paid a small fortune to have never wandered up that side street.

I paid up and quickly walked off with my prize, immediately feeling guilty for robbing a couple of poor old souls. I am an atheist but nevertheless I fear that The Fist will come and clobber me after every act of meanness I commit – and it usually does in some form or other. Stuffing the phone into a plastic carrier bag helped hide away my guilt.

After hardly a quarter of an hour I could not live with my conscience any longer and so I retraced my steps to the side street intent of returning to the old couple and handing over the extra thirty Euros I had cheated them out of. I found the street easily enough but not the stallholders. The *vide grenier* had hardly gotten into its stride and yet they appeared to have scarpered already. How about that?

Halfway down the main street I caught Patrick coming back towards me. He was carrying a bag full of "finds" and with a stuffed hind's head under his free arm. "I've bought more gear so I'll have to go back for the rest. Will you give me a hand?" Taking that for granted and so not waiting for a reply he asked, "Did you find anything?"

"Just an old telephone." Patrick probably did not hear what I had said; he was too focussed on his own merchandise.

We had to make three journeys back to a dozen or so destinations in order to gather up Patrick's booty. The worst was a two hundred or so litre oval barrel that had seen better days and smelled horribly inside of vinegar. "The money's in that little enamel label on the side which reads 'CIDRE' and in its oval shape," explained my companion.

I gave no thought to my purchase until we had returned to Patrick's place. In the hall pulled out the telephone from its bag and nonchalantly place it on a convenient table. Patrick fairly jumped forward and picked it up. I thought that he was going to scold me for risking scratching his precious table. "Where did you get this?" he demanded.

I related my story.

"Thirty Euros eh? You've done well. Of course it's pretty well knackered but I'll give you a profit on it. I've a customer for old telephones and similar stuff."

"What sort of profit Patrick?" I had no qualms about selling the telephone to him but relished a bit of fun first; to play him at his own game perhaps.

"I'll double your money."

"No."

"O.K. a ton then?"

In other circumstances I would probably have accepted a hundred Euros and been pleased with the instant profit. If I had had half an inkling of what that instrument had in store for me I would have given Patrick money, loads of money, to take it from out of my hands. But I didn't and at that particular moment I let Patrick, in my terminology, stew in his own juice. No doubt he would have another pop at me prior to my departure back to Blighty the following morning.

Before we loaded the cider press and mill into my van that afternoon I made the point of paying Patrick the full nine hundred Euros in cash. I didn't want him arguing the toss or, even worse, Madame weighing in with her two centimes. That done, hands shaken, I felt a lot happier and Patrick insisted that we enjoyed a drop of Irish whiskey together in a bolt hole he had engineered in a corner of one of the stables.

"I only drink Irish to keep up the myth," he confided. "I much prefer Scotch. My dad was an Orangeman but Evette doesn't know that. You'll keep my confidence won't you Des?"

I nodded.

"He wouldn't have anything to do with them south of the border. Hated them he did. Silly old fucker."

"You weren't born in the Republic then?"

"No, I have a British passport but that is O.K. with Evette, me being a Celt. Although I wouldn't like to put that to the test of a genealogical investigation."

"No, I suppose we would all get some shocks if the truth were told," I agreed.

"Now what about this telephone, Des? Are you going to sell it to me?"

"What's it really worth Patrick?"

The man seemed to tussle with his conscience and then surprised me with the outcome. "I don't rightly know, Des, I've got more than enough money and I don't need to con you out of your prize. You take it back home with you as a smart memento of your trip here. Far better than a plastic model of St. Michael's Mount."

I came down to dinner that evening to an empty room. I knew that the Dutch couple had left because we had said our good-byes the evening before. The French foursome might have been trying to tell me of their departure too but the sentiment could have failed to percolate through the language barrier. The meal was scratchy and served by Patrick in person; obviously the staff's day off. He made up for the shortcoming by providing me with a complimentary bottle of good red wine.

I was sitting back, sated, slightly tipsy, idly studying the gothic numerals on the face of the Vienna clock when I heard a scream out in the hall. The time was eight fifty-seven. As any decent bloke would, I hurried out to investigate to find that Patrick had beaten me to the source of the clamour. That being Evette, I was rather glad that he had. The woman was clearly distressed and rabbiting volubly in her native tongue. The only word that I could pick out was *sonner*, or something similar; no mean feat considering the way she was shrieking.

Patrick embraced his wife desperately trying to console her before gently leading her through a door into their private quarters. Turning to me in the process he said, "It's O.K. Des. You go back and finish your meal and I'll be with you in a minute."

That minute proved to be the best part of an hour. I had emptied the bottle of wine and was on the point of making my way up to my bedroom when Patrick appeared holding a bottle of Irish and a pair of tumblers into which he poured large measures. "You take this neat don't you?" without waiting for an answer. "Phew, I don't know what that was all about."

"What's upset her?" I said, asking the obvious question.

"She says that telephone of your rang three times; three long rings as French telephones do. How could it? There are no wires to connect it to the system. There's no bell in the base – it's a physical impossibility. Evette knows that, she's no fool, yet she is adamant that it rang." He took a second big slug of the amber liquid. "It's a bloody mystery Desmond. She is highly strung by nature, and has been overdoing things lately but this is a definite first."

"Did she lift the handset?"

"Yes, the silly cow did it automatically. Evidently a voice said 'bonjour, bonjour'. Yvette flipped totally and slammed the receiver down. I've tried it and of course the thing's as dead as a dodo. I reckon she's having one of her funny turns – she gets them now and again."

"That's all she heard?" I asked.

"Yes." He paused thoughtfully. "She said it was a man's voice speaking urgently. And, although she heard only those two words he didn't sound French."

"Not French?"

"The whole thing's preposterous"

"Is there anything I can do to help?" I asked in an attempt at sympathy.

"Yes, there is. Take that fucking phone upstairs with you or, better still, stick it in your van." As an afterthought he added, "Please."

The following morning I departed in darkness in order to get to the ferry port by 0700hrs. Quite likely I would have failed a breathalyser but I saw neither hide nor hair of the gendarmerie. Patrick came to wave me off in a designer dressing gown. Unsurprisingly Madame Laignel did not deign to wish me *bon voyage*.

His parting words to me were, "Got the telephone in the van, Des?"

CHAPTER THREE

"Looks like a tump of shite to me," offered Old Sam after a cursory inspection of the van's cargo.

Having been on the road for three hours after driving up from Portsmouth I was not in the mood to bandy insults with him. "Just give me a hand unloading will you, Sam." He was not much help except with the two heaviest pieces; the press base and the mill. He grunted and groaned and scowled much as I had expected him to but he was surprisingly strong for an old man. Eventually the whole kit and kaboodle was piled up on the grassy orchard floor and darkness had fallen.

"You're not going to leave that there, is you?"

"Why not?" I replied. "Nobody is likely to run off with it."

"Don't be so sure. Nice drop of firewood; it'll burn lovely"

"It'll be O.K. where it is, especially if it rains. Needs a good soaking." I picked my travel bag from out of the cab and Sam followed me into the cottage. "I've brought you back a present, Sam." I grinned, depositing two bottles of French dry *cidre* onto the kitchen table.

"*Brut*, what's that about?" asked Sam grumpily reading from a label.

"Dry. Dry cider." I twisted off the champagne type wires and eased off the cork which made a reassuring "plop" as the pressure was released from inside. I then poured a small taster into a glass and held it out to the old man. I had never noticed before the amount of hairs growing out of his nostrils. His face grimaced worse that it had done outside in the orchard. "What do you think Sam?"

"T'aint as good as 'Ereford cider. This ere's fizzy pop."

Fizzy pop or not, there were no prizes in guessing as to who had the lion's share of the contents of both bottles which disappeared in double quick time. "Did yer bring any more back?" Sam started clicking his tongue and sniffing which were sure signs that the alcohol was taking effect.

"That depends."

"On what?" questioned Sam, looking hopeful.

"On whether you help me set up the cider press tomorrow."

"Hmmmm." he said, noncommittally.

"I'll tell you what, Sam, I'll go and get a jug up from the cellar."

The old man shuffled in his chair, guilt written all over his face. "There ain't any left."

"What," I exclaimed. "There was nearly a full keg last Thursday." I had purchased a five gallon plastic barrel of unfiltered cider only the previous Wednesday. Sam looked as sheepish as any one of his four legged protégés from a working life spent, for the most part, as a Radnorshire shepherd.

. "Have you brought some of your cronies here from the Tap Room of the Dog and Duck?"

"Only Barney Bates. I needed 'im to 'elp get the stuff up from below."

That sounded about right as I knew of Sam's aversion to descending the steps down into my cellar. "Where's the empty barrel?"

"Outside."

"I think that I can count on your help for more than just tomorrow, Sam."

"Appen," the apparently contrite cadger assented.

"I did bring back something else." Sam's hopeful gleam evaporated when I pulled the telephone from out of my travel bag. Nevertheless he deigned to examine the instrument closely.

"That'll never work."

"I could have it converted perhaps." I put the telephone on the kitchen dresser.

Before he departed Sam offered some free advice. "You'd better get your arse in gear. There's more to cider making than sclemming an old press and talking about the job in 'and. What are you going to ferment the juice in? And where? Anyways, I'll come round tomorrow and gives you an 'and with putting the Frenchie together."

"Make it the afternoon, Sam, I have to take this van back to the hire people and collect my car"

The following morning the sky was overcast, the low cloud mirroring my spirits especially after I observed the remains of a bottle of Speyside malt. "It wasn't so much the whisky," I told myself, "but the mixing it with cider." Black coffee served to restore my humour somewhat.

Lo and behold, Peter the salesman bounced out to meet me almost before I could set a foot on the forecourt of Rillington's Garage. He greeted me effusively as if we had known each other from schooldays. In contrast I exhibited more than a touch of frost. "Eight hundred Euros your mate Patrick wanted for the press – not the three hundred that you led me to believe."

Peter was not fazed in the slightest. "Blow me, that old rogue Patrick, I never could trust him. He'd say anything, swap his old grandmother and the rest. You can't trust the Irish."

"He's more English than I am," I said, not knowing what to believe. I felt like a herring in a pool of sharks.

By the time that Peter had scrutinised the van for scratches or worse, and we had completed the paperwork I had elicited a promise from him that he would sacrifice part of his week-end to help with cider making. I supposed that, providing he kept his word, free labour would go a little way to ameliorating the cost of the French equipment.

That afternoon Sam turned up as promised but rather later than expected. I should have guessed that he would have called into the Dog and Duck for a "couple of harns". We assembled the press by trial and error and a wealth of negativity from my pensioner companion. "You needs to get some tarpaulins to put on the ground else it'll get as kludgy as a byre. And what about fermenters? Them what you needs to puts the juice in."

Wednesday saw me chasing down "fermenters". By a tedious series of networking I discovered a chap at the Cider Museum who tipped me off that I could buy whisky casks from a firm in Evesham. These turned out to be straight from a bottling plant in Glasgow and between the four that I purchased came an unexpected bonus. I was able to drain off nearly half a pint of malt whisky strong enough to blow a man's head off. I was obliged to make two tedious journeys from Well Cottage to Evesham to collect two casks at a time in my small car and during which the whisky fumes were enough to make me giddy. With a capacity of about 250 litres each, or so I was assured, I should have more than enough capacity.

Thursday morning saw me clearing out the garage at Well Cottage in order to make space for an improvised fermenting room. In the afternoon I started collecting apples from off the floor of the orchard. The previous night had been windy and as a result the windfalls appeared to have trebled, there being far more on the ground than left on the trees as far as I could judge. I had seen many romantic pictures of families happily picking up apples in weak Autumn sunlight, but on a cold, windy day, after just an hour, my back and thighs ached past the point of toleration. I managed another half hour or so by kneeling on a plastic bag but after that I gave up and resorted to raking apples into tidy piles.

Friday was spent collecting more fruit until I became exhausted again. As a relief I drove off to purchase some large terylene sheets from a builder's merchant, some plastic bowls and buckets, four air locks for the whisky casks and another two five gallon kegs of cloudy cider. By teatime everything seemed to be in place for an industrious start the following morning.

Alas, Saturday was a complete wash-out; it rained cats and dogs all day, and there was no sign of Sam, not even at teatime (cider-time to him). I spent the day doing household chores and checking the state of the weather through the cottage's small windows. Come evening I couldn't even be bothered to sidle down to the Dog and Duck and decided to watch some television instead.

Thank goodness Sunday dawned bright and dry. The orchard was filled with the heady perfume of rotting and fermenting apples and the buzz-buzz of attendant wasps above the last notes of the fading dawn chorus. Sam shuffled in through the field gate in an even older brown raincoat held in place by orange baling twine the like of which would have had a scarecrow turn up its nose.

I filled the hopper with apples whilst Sam turned the handle of the mill and soon we had a growing pile of mush that was beginning to leak juice. This we took turns into shovelling into plastic buckets to unload into the press nearby. Come mid-morning, when the press was just about full Peter came whistling along, dressed immaculately as ever in what he would describe as 'designer' work gear complete with two-tone green Wellington boots.

The rain of the previous day had understandably made the ground sodden and where Sam and I had walked outside the plastic sheeting was a muddy morass. Peter viewed this with distaste and tip-toed through trying to keep the soiling of his boots to the minimum. The look on Sam's wizened face was priceless. No doubt the wisest course of action was to put Pete on pressing duties.

A little juice started trickling between the oak slats of the press during the drawn out loading process but as soon as the wooden top plate was secured and the iron bar used as a lever, slotted into the gearing mechanism, a fair stream of juice oozed out. The liquid collected in the base and trickled out of the spout filling a plastic bucket strategically placed on the floor.

"Hey, slow down there," shouted Sam. "If you puts too much pressure too soon you push out loads of mush. 'Tis the juice you want. Turn a bit and stop. Then turn a bit then stop. Keep taking the juice to the barrels down yonder." Peter did as he was instructed and for a good while all three of us were absorbed in our industry.

I provided a scratch lunch of wholemeal bread, cheese and pickle which we all washed down with fresh apple juice. Sam muttered that he would have preferred the fermented version to no avail. I was amazed at the sweetness of the juice. Previously, wandering through my newly acquired orchard, I had bitten into many of the different apple varieties discovering a very few to be sweetish and marginally palatable whilst most of them sour and sharp. Almost all were dry to the mouth. Not only was I pleasantly surprised as to how relatively sweet the newly pressed juice tasted but also the amount of liquid that emanated from the apples. That was just another revelation that added to the magic of the day.

By teatime I fully appreciated why the boys of yore collected round a barrel of cider and passed round the horn from one to another. The intoxicating smells of orchard and the pressing process combined with the weariness of intensive physical labour, spiced with camaraderie, engendered a mighty thirst for the finished product. Although it was a new plastic cask standing on the kitchen table, and we each had our own tumblers to drink from rather than a horn to pass between us, we paid deference to the days of yore.

We were too tired and self-satisfied to talk overmuch. I remember glancing up at the kitchen clock, seeing that eight o'clock was approaching, and thinking that I ought to offer my fellow workers some food, when the silence was shattered by a piercing ring…ring…ring. Not the double ring of the British system but the single ring of the French.

If I had not been befuddled with alcohol and tiredness I might have metaphorically jumped out of my skin. It was as though someone other than me was passively sitting where I was, looking across at the French telephone on the dresser, and thinking it was perfectly natural and logical. Perhaps Sam's dropped jaw and wide-eyed stare prompted me to reach across, pick the whole instrument up and place it on the table before lifting the handset.

«*Bonjour, bonjour, aidez-moi s'il vous plait, aidez…*»

"You what?" I interrupted instinctively. . Silly though it was they were the first words that came to mind.

"You speak English?" said the voice hesitantly.

Although this happened in a split second a picture flashed through my mind that this was some elaborate joke contrived by that bastard Patrick. I had mused about the so-called incident with Evette and in my list of possibilities I had not ruled out a wind-up just for my benefit.

"Actually Patrick, I'm fucking Welsh," I sneered as a rejoinder to Evette's dislike of the English and his laboured Irishness.

"No, no, you have to believe me, sir, I'm Flight Lieutenant Jaman K. Ricci," the voice reeled off a series of numbers "and I need help."

"Nice one Patrick. I like your American accent."

"Listen buddy, I told you, my names Ricci, R-I-C-C-I." He spelled out his surname tersely; stress evident in his voice. "You with the Germans?"

"The Germans?" I gasped, doubts creeping in that this had nothing to do with Patrick after all. I was still too caught up for the jitters to properly creep in. "Who the fuck are you?"

"Don't snap your cap buddy, there ain't time enough. Where are you?"

"Here in England."

"In England?" The surprise in the voice was evident. There was a pause and then, "Tell my base in Nosterham, tell them NOW, please, that I am down near the copper town – they'll know what I mean. In an old quarry. Tell them that my bird took…"

The line went suddenly silent as if there never had been a conversation. I put the receiver gently back on its cradle.

"That's a fine piece of role play," laughed Peter, "Was it for my benefit?"

"No role play Pete." My hands were shaking as the realisation took charge. I told my two companions what I had just heard.

I have never seen Sam move so fast. Normally he almost shuffled from point A to point B, his slight frame hunched. That day he was out of the door and gone at the trot leaving a half empty glass, something unheard of.

"You're telling me that there was REALLY a voice on the line? You expect me to believe that?" asked Peter incredulously.

"I swear it on the Bible."

"I bet you're an atheist."

"You happen to be correct so I'll swear it on Satan's arsehole instead," I rejoined testily trying to control the shakes.

We went through what had been said several times, and then some more. Peter took the telephone and using one of my screwdrivers expertly dismantled the base until the instrument was laid bare. There were no clever electronics that took the form of a wireless receiver – nothing at all that was not original to the telephone. So what could have made the ringing sound let alone the voice? There was no denying that Peter had heard the ring tone – as had Sam for that matter.

We talked ourselves into silence. I was now calm and we both had sobered up considerably.

"Tell you what, I'll give Patrick a ring." Peter looked at his mobile. "There's no signal in here." I could have told him that." I'll try out on the lane. Whilst I'm there write everything down on paper while it's still fresh in your mind."

I fetched paper and pen and made the appropriate notes which did not amount to much. As an afterthought I added the date and time and then it struck me that the telephone call had been exactly a week after the one that Evette received. Adjusting for the time differential between the U.K. and France the time was exact to the minute as far as I was aware. Was that just a coincidence? Surely not.

Peter was away for over twenty minutes in his search for a signal on his mobile and when he did eventually appear his face was one of puzzlement. "Pat swears on his life and those of his unborn children, what he said to you was the absolute truth. For what it's worth I believe him."

"Wow," was all I could manage.

"I promised that we would not breathe a word of this to Evette."

"Fat chance of my doing so."

"You made notes?" asked Peter authoritatively.

"Yes."

"Let me see." He read what I had scribbled down. "Nosterham, have you heard of such a place?"

"Search me. If such a place is in Britain I have a very good road map with an index." I found it straight away in the bookcase in the lounge and brought it back with me to the kitchen. Sure enough there was an entry for Nosterham and a page and location reference. Another few minutes and I had my finger on a small village of that name. "Nearest town is Tunbridge Wells I would guess."

"Royal Tunbridge Wells," corrected Peter dryly and quite unnecessarily. "That's a morsel of authenticity I suppose."

"He said that he is, or was, a Flight Lieutenant and his bird came down near Copper Town and to tell his base in Nosterham. He had a marked American accent and his name is something Ricci. I didn't get his first name except that I thought that it started with the letter 'J'. What chance a U.S. airfield at this place Nosterham?"

"Who knows," answered Peter thoughtfully. "We aren't going to suss that one out tonight. But we ought to take another good look at the telephone instrument. Just in case we missed something.""

I tentatively approached the sideboard and lifted the phone gingerly to place it on the table before Peter again. I hardly liked to admit to myself that I was glad to be able to delegate a detailed examination to my companion. Peter had no such qualms apparently and manhandled the machine brusquely. He made notes whilst I made coffee.

"Each of the three pieces has different maker's plate giving plenty of information about its history. Not the sort of detail that you get these days. The main caste iron part was made on the 10th March 1937, the Bakelite hand piece made by a Paris firm in 1928 and the matching ear piece by a different Paris maker in December 1934. There are serial numbers and a reference to the phone being a model introduced in 1924. There was originally an exchange number written at the centre of the dial but it's illegible. There is no ringing mechanism. Unless technology has taken giant strides that I know nothing about, then there is no way that the instrument could fulfil the function that it was designed to do. It's a complete sodding mystery to me."

We sat mulling over the conundrum for a good while until Peter suggested we "bugger off to the Dog and Duck and get thoroughly rat-arsed." Sitting in the lounge bar we didn't talk much; we were both in our own worlds mulling over Flight Lieutenant J. Ricci. Drink, however, we did manage and Peter snored in my spare room for the best part of the night.

In the morning I was obliged to arrange a taxi for my guest. Peter was not as foolhardy about breathalysers as I had been on my return leg up through Normandy that previous Monday. He didn't look quite as dapper as was his custom with bleary eyes and a nasty dried cut from one of my cheap razors. His shoes too had forfeited much of their shine. I took care to dose him up with half a bucket of black coffee. His last words to me from the back of the taxi were, "I'll see what I can find out about Nosterham."

When my brain had started to function properly and send clear commands to my legs, I went to check our profit from the previous day in the fermenting room a.k.a. my garage. The glass airlocks on the two full ex-whisky barrels were bubbling away merrily whilst the third, temporarily occupying the bung hole of the part filled barrel, was also showing the escape of carbon dioxide. From this I took a sample using a pipette that I had also purchased earlier in the week, and transferred it to a small glass. Expecting the liquid to taste as delicious as the raw juice had done the day before, I was disappointed. Just a few hours of fermentation had altered the taste radically – and to its detriment.

I spent the remainder of the morning alternating between collecting apples from off the orchard floor and cleaning the equipment ready for the next cider making operation. Somewhere along the line an idea occurred to me. I would put to one side, that afternoon, apples from the Ten Commandments and Yarlington Mill varieties. Hadn't Sam said on the first day that I had met him, that those two made a very good cider?. Besides, they were the only two varieties that I knew by name.

Peter telephoned me as I was preparing my lunch.

"I contacted an acquaintance who has a good knowledge of the R.A.F. during W.W.2. He is sure that RAF Nosterham was a USAAF base in the war, principally for the 354 Fighter Group who were equipped with Mustangs. P51 Mustangs to be precise. Initially they were used to protect American bombers over Germany but pre and post D-Day they flew many operations over the Northern France. They were capable of long range flights evidently."

"Is Nosterham still used as an airfield did you ask?"

"Yes, I did. It was purely a wartime thing. Now it's back to ploughed fields and a modern housing estate."

"Wow, haven't you done well," I said at a loss of something better to say.

"He had no idea as to what 'copper town' could be. I'll have to work on that one. Must go…"

Up to that point the improbable ringing of the telephone and the conversation that had ensued were surreal, to say the least, and with Peter's pragmatism and a drenching of cider no doubt, I had felt relatively calm. But the verification that Nosterham, a place that I had never heard of to my knowledge, was in fact a wartime USAAF base , caused a wave of emotion within me. Shaking legs and hands obliged me to abandon my luncheon preparations and take refuge in an armchair. Then, as now, I am not the bravest of souls.

I needed to tell someone, the authorities, but whom? A whole range of possibilities crossed my mind. But all lines ended in buffers; who was going to believe me? I did have Peter for corroboration . He did not hear both sides of the telephone conversation though and proof would ultimately come down to my word. After maybe an hour of mental fidgeting I came to the conclusion to wait and see whether the telephone would ring again and to try and get Peter, or anyone else involved if that should occur again.

By mid-week I had lifted all the apples on the ground in the orchard and had to resort to shaking branches with a clothes line prop. I had hoped that Sam might sidle along and give me a hand milling and pressing but the events on Sunday evening must have spooked him to such an extent that he forwent his liberal doses of free cider. On Thursday Peter telephoned to arrange a rendezvous in the Dog and Duck for that evening along with a promise to turn up for another session of cider making the coming Sunday.

In the meantime I reckoned that I had enough apples tumped up to more than fill the part barrel and the empty one too. I would need more capacity in which to ferment the juice of the double varietal cider I intended making from the Yarlingtons and the Ten Commandments. Accordingly I went into town and found four ten gallon plastic containers made for the job at a shop specialising in home brew beers and wines. From a potato merchant I bought some paper sacks to further an idea fermenting in my mind; I would try selling my surplus apples to Bulmers.

Peter just beat me into the lounge bar of the Dog and Duck. I had a quick peep into the tiny Tap Room on the way just to see if Sam was sitting in his favourite corner gassing with the other old codgers. He was, and pretended not to see me. Crafty old bugger.

"I've news for you, my son," said Peter excitedly. So excitedly in fact that he omitted to order me a pint. He sat on his bar stool impatiently whilst I rectified the situation and watched my favourite barmaid, Emma, demurely work the beer engine. "I've been onto the American Air Museum at Duxford. I asked about a Flight Lieutenant called J.K.Ricci based at RAF Nosterham. They took down the details and said that I would have to wait a month or so whilst their researchers found the time to trawl through the records. I convinced them it was extremely urgent…"

"You didn't tell them about the phone call, did you?" I interrupted disapprovingly.

"No, no, what do you take me for? I gave them the close relative on their death bed story – usually works."

"You salesmen have few morals," I interrupted again.

"Do you want to know Des, or don't you? "

"Of course I do."

"Stop moralising then. Duxford came back to me within forty-eight hours. There was a Flight Lieutenant Jaman K. Ricci – Jamie to his friends – whose P51 Mustang went missing over France a few days before D-Day. What do you make of that?" he blurted excitedly.

No wonder he'd been bursting to tell me. I really didn't know what to make of the information. My body was not similarly confused judging by the chill travelling down my spine.

"He went missing on the 3rd June 1944, three days before D-Day. He had been on a mission in Lower Normandy charged with shooting up freight trains in the St. Lo area. He wouldn't have known it but the idea was to cause as much disruption to the German war machine just prior to the invasion. He also didn't know that he was scheduled to provide air cover for the fleet of gliders that would be in the vanguard of Operation Neptune."

"And copper town?"

"My contact at Duxford couldn't help with that one. Nothing jumped out of their records."

"Do they know where he went down?"

"No, not a thing. There was no Mayday or whatever they called a distress signal. He was flying solo so none of his comrades saw anything nor were there ever any verifiable reports from people on the ground. His disappearance is, and was, a total mystery. That's unusual I'm told. Apart from the U.S. authorities there is a lot of interest generally in marking, recording and preserving crash sites and especially so when there are missing airmen involved".

Peter babbled on. "They knew quite a bit about Jamal – I'll call him Jamie – because of his Italian background. He joined the U.S. Army – their air personnel are part of the Army – whilst Italy was still the enemy. Before Mussolini was hanged that is. He was born in Italy before his parents emigrated to America when he was a baby. Because he held dual passports there were questions about his loyalty. Anyway, that was resolved and he proved his worth with two kills and one probable to his name. He was brought up in a place called… Just a sec." Peter felt in his jacket pocket and brought out a slip of paper which he studied. "Plumwood. It's a small commune evidently, in Ohio, thirty miles or so west of Columbus. What do you think of that?"

I had been studying the mirror-like toecaps of Peter's shoes without seeing them, as it were. What did I think of that? A mixture of fear, foreboding, anxiety, uncertainty as what to do next? I honestly cannot remember. Yet there must have been a tingle of excitement too.

I do remember saying to Peter after a long pause, "This is not going to go away."

CHAPTER FOUR

On Friday evening Sam turned up at tea-time on his usual scrounge trying to act as though everything was back to normal, with things as they had been before the telephone call. I lambasted him in fun on a charge of desertion and was horrified to witness him cower and bare his teeth in a submissive grin just like I imagined a whipped dog might do. I quickly proceeded to restore normality by explaining my charge was in jest.

"The penalty for going AWOL," I put to the old shepherd with a warm smile, "is to help me make some special cider tomorrow using those Ten Commandments mixed with Yarlington Mills or any other varieties you can recognise and think suitable. And if you help again on Sunday I'll pay you by the hour."

"What, in cider, like the olden days?"

"No Sam, in money. The cider afterwards will be free." I wanted to add "as ever".

Sitting at the kitchen table with the first drop of cider down his scrawny gullet, Sam was soon much his old self. Reaching into the shabbiness of his raincoat pocket he muttered. "I've brought 'ee a present." Out came a smallish black and white furry ball which transformed itself into a wide-eyed kitten desperately trying to regain its equilibrium in the strange environment of my table.

I thought, "What a sweet little thing." What I said was, "And you can take that right back where it came from."

"Can't do that Gaffer. There was four of 'em in a bin bag barely afloat in the river. Three dead uns and 'im, barely alive. I dried him off and put 'im in my coat pocket and 'ees perked up a mite." By this time the kitten was meowing pathetically and noisily. "He wants a bite to eat," observed Sam dispassionately.

"It needs its mother," I suggested realising pretty quickly that was unrealistic.

"Naw, it's weaned. Eight or nine weeks old I'd say. That's when they drown them – when they starts costing money."

I obliged the animal with bread saturated in a saucer of milk and was duly rewarded by the enthusiasm with which the mixture was received. "I can't take on a kitten, Sam. I…"

I was about to embark on a long list of reasons but Sam cut me short. "Just for tonight Gaffer." Suddenly I had become 'Gaffer'. "You can take kitty to the cat's home in the morning."

"I can take him?"

"You've got a car. I'd 'ave to get the bus and it only runs on Wednesday and Saturdays. Besides, you want me to help you tomorrow. Corse, I could take the bus into town but the one back ain't 'till teatime."

Game, set and match to Sam. "How do you know it's a he?" I asked lamely.

"It's an 'E alright. I knows these things. Can I have another swallow of that there cider, Gaffer?"

Later, after Sam had swayed off into the night, I was sitting in the lounge reading about cider making when I heard a kerfuffle from the direction of the kitchen. On investigation I found the kitten had discovered a bottle cap, presumably from underneath the dresser, and was enjoying a great game batting it with a front paw and then chasing it across the stone slabs of the kitchen's floor. I must have watched for a good five minutes, occasional kicking the 'ball' back into play as and when it came into the range of my shoe.

Eventually I returned to the lounge, picked up my book and continued reading from where I had left off. Soon after I saw kitty wandering in the room from the corner of my eye, committed no doubt to exploring my territory. The next interruption was his inability to jump up and join me. I relented and lifted him onto the sofa beside me. Not content with that the little pest clawed his way up my arm and sat on my shoulder, tickling my ear with his tiny whiskers, and seemingly pretending to read the book with me. If the cat was trying to endear himself to me he was making exactly the right moves in order to achieve that objective.

I had no history of cat ownership and therefore my knowledge of the species was somewhat sketchy, but over the next hour or so, I became convinced that the kitten's age was in doubt and that Sam's story of an attempted drowning was a fallacy. That was a conundrum that needed to be explored on the morrow. My bedtime saw kitty secured in the kitchen, a sheet of newspaper spread on the floor, a cushion in a corner and an empty tin of sardines in the waste bin.

Saturday dawned crisp and bright and I entered the kitchen with some trepidation. I need not have worried. Kitty's head uncurled from his cushion to award me a welcoming, silent meow. What cemented my delight was observing a wet patch and a small element of poo almost precisely positioned in the centre of the newspaper ."What a clever cat you are," I murmured involuntarily giving him a rewarding stroke. Within the hour I could be found at the village shop purchasing sachets of kitten food.

Sam sidled in mid-morning, looking shifty. His eyes did not meet mine but readily took in the empty dish next to a fresh sheet of newsprint. He wasn't then to know that the kitten was curled up asleep on my sofa, its small stomach satisfactorily extended. "Nice day for making cider, Sam," I greeted him.

"You're right on the button there, Gaffer," he replied, his shoulders relaxing somewhat. "Shall we make a start?" I was minded to give him some dog's abuse about the kitten, but what was the point? I pretty well knew what his reaction would be and I am no bully at heart. Besides, I was not as adamant as I had been about delivering the wee scrap to the nearest animal rescue centre. Making cider would be a good excuse to delay that decision.

I left Sam working in the corner of the orchard where the equipment was set up whilst I went into Hereford to buy two more ten gallon containers and appropriate air locks from the home-brewing shop. The four that I had previously purchased had been treated to a disdainful scowl by my cider maker-in-chief. I also took the opportunity to pop into a pet shop to buy cat litter and tray and some more kitten food. I kidded myself that I was not bonding with kitty – just making his temporary stay more convivial for both of us.

Cider making with Sam was so physically exhausting that Saturday that I gave hardly a thought to the telephone on the dresser or the mysterious call from Jamie Ricci. That was to be rectified when I met Peter as arranged in the Dog and Duck in the evening. He was bursting with fresh news.

"Duxford rang me this morning. Evidently my researcher, her name's Janice Farmer, is a part-time volunteer and does not always have access to the archives mid-week. She's dug up a report from a Resistance worker in Villedeau-les-Poeles dated 5.6.1944. Villedeau is famous for making things in copper. Has to be Jamie's "copper town".

"Sounds likely," I agreed.

"The Germans had set up a mobile Ack-Ack battery on the outskirts of Villedeau and an observer on the ground reported that the day before, the 4th June, he had witnessed a lone American fighter aircraft disappearing southwards leaving a smoke trail. It is likely that the aircraft sustained a direct hit."

"No suggestion of a parachute?"

"No. Evidently the Resistance man's view was obstructed by buildings. The USAAF records tentatively tied the sighting to Ricci's disappearance but nothing further came to light and this was just another of thousands of incidents."

We chatted on, making no further headway with our mystery. "You want to stay the night, Peter, as you're committed to some cider making tomorrow?"

"Might as well. I've got my working gear in the car."

The kitten won Peter over straight away and in the morning too, nestling in his lap at the breakfast table. I surprised myself by feeling a touch of jealousy rising. When Peter asked the cat's name I blurted out "Denzil". Why on earth did I do that?

"I wouldn't mind taking him home with me," said my guest, more to the kitten than to me.

"No chance," I breathed. I swear that Denzil looked up at me that precise moment and smiled.

"Blimey, is that Sam out there?" asked Peter looking through the kitchen window. "He's bloody keen. What's got into him I wonder?"

I wondered too. Sam just treated me to an enigmatic half smile and hardly paused from milling a mixture of Yarlington Mills and Ten Commandments to acknowledge my greeting. Head down, his disgustingly filthy flat cap, which I would rarely see him without, hid his eyes and prevented me from reading his face. Fine chance I had of doing that anyway. He just carried on with his work, slow and steady, as if to set an example to us two greenhorns – Peter and me.

The day was overcast and chilly but Peter and I only noticed the cold when we stopped for a tea break. By late afternoon I was delighted to survey four full wooden whisky barrels and six plastic kegs, all surmounted with glass airlocks showing signs of virgin bubbles. They were lined up importantly in my improvised fermenting room. As we re-assembled in my kitchen I offered my guests the use of my shower. Whilst Peter accepted with alacrity Sam remained firmly seated close to the warm Aga, a glass of cider welded into his gnarled fingers. I guessed that showering was not part of his personal hygiene routine.

I had had the foresight to prepare a huge chicken casserole the previous evening which had been simmering in the bottom oven of the Aga for most of the day. Having showered myself and after feeding a silently meowing Denzil, we three wolfed down the stew, proof there is nothing like physical exercise and fresh air to stimulate the appetite. All the while, however, Peter and I caste nervous glances at the clock. Sam was oblivious to our expectation that if the French telephone was going to ring then a shade before eight o'clock would be the likely time.

Sure enough, that was what happened. On the second ring two of us stood up, me in a movement towards the instrument sitting on the dresser and Sam heading straight for the back door. In his hurry to escape, Sam's chair overturned backwards and hit the floor with such a clatter that Denzil flew straight upwards , four legs rigid and tail ceiling-wise as straight as a poker.

I lifted the receiver before the fourth ring aware that Peter was moving across the room to join me. He had the separate ear-piece off its cradle and to his right ear before the caller spoke.

"Hello?" I asked shakily, clearing my throat in the process.

"Help me, help me," came a voice that I instantly recognised.

"You're Flight Lieutenant Jamal Ricci of 345 Fighter Group out of Nosterham, right?"

"Right, sir." The voice sounded surprised. "But how did you know that?"

"And your plane was hit by flack over Villedeau-les-Poeles?" If the conversation was to be anything like the first time I knew that I had to hurry. No time for niceties.

"Sure buddy, right on the button. Copper town."

"Where are you?"

"… under water."

"Where did you crash?" I surprised myself at my directness.

"There was a humdinger of a bang behind the cockpit. Lost height and looking for somewhere to land the bird. Small fields with hedges everywhere. Sweet Jesus, a long straight road ahead. I'm gonna make it."

"You didn't make it?" I asked.

"What direction were you flying in?" interrupted Peter pushing me from the mouthpiece sufficient to be cheek by cheek.

The line went quiet. For a second I thought that the call had ended as abruptly as the previous one had. Rather, the second question and the new voice had either put Ricci on his guard or confused him.

"…err, south-easterly I guess."

"What happened?" I regained control of the instrument.

"Peeled off to the right, nosedived into a circle of trees. Big pond in centre. Splash. Help me. Help me." The wavering voice trailed off.

At that the line went totally dead. Peter barged in again and shouted into the mouthpiece but to no avail.

A wave of emotion flooded through my body and I was glad to sit back down at the kitchen table. Peter's reaction was to pace back and forth, repeatedly muttering the words spoken during that short communication – Ricci's and ours. After a while we retired to the lounge and saw off half a bottle of scotch between us. Increasingly Peter dominated the conversation, going over and over the words spoken and drawing inferences that became wilder and more improbable as the liquid level in the bottle dropped.

The next thing that I knew was a loud purring in my left ear and whiskers spasmodically tickling my face. My bleary eyes concentrated on the mantle clock and two-thirty-five eventually came into focus. A long day spent cider-making in the fresh air and the soporific effects of the whisky had taken their toll and I had apparently dropped off with Peter in mid-sentence. Denzil must have clawed his way up my outstretched leg. I gently imprisoned him in the kitchen and clambered up the winding stairs, checking the guest bedroom before I crashed out. Peter was snoring soundly, fully clothed on top of the duvet.

When I awoke the clock on my mobile phone read 09.43. Phew, that was the longest and most refreshing sleep that I had had in years. But when I moved aches and pains in my legs, arms and back reminded me unkindly of the previous day's toil. The guest bedroom was empty, the duvet neatly folded back in place. Peter must have left early in order to get to his flat in the centre of Hereford in time to make himself immaculate for his working day.

Denzil, incarcerated in the kitchen, greeted me with a gentle purring. Peter had evidently fed him for, although his dish had been licked clean, the wee animal's stomach was comfortingly distended and the kitten was obviously intent on mischief and play.

I glared at the French telephone on the sideboard on more than a few occasions that day and several times resisted a temptation to put it away in a cupboard, out of sight. Somehow that would have been a defeat and I was not in a mood for such a concession. The day passed with my paying compensation to my aches and pains and doing very little. Probably the highlight was standing in the fermenting room and watching the bubbles escape with increasing momentum from the ten glass airlocks. I remembered the boy that was my youth, planting radish seeds, my first attempt to be a son of the soil, and being impatient for them to grow to the point that I gave up. That was not going to happen with my cider enterprise – no way.

Sam came and went and came again the next day – and went. He didn't mention the telephone and neither did I. I caught his brown eyes glowering at the instrument darkly from under his grease encrusted flat cap a few times, but that was the sum total of his disinterest. Conversely he took great delight in the embryo cider in the garage and a lengthy inspection became his daily routine as he assumed the role of cidermaker-in-chief.

"A dead rat in one of them barrels would give it a bit of body," he joked. At least I hoped that he was joking.

"I'm sorry, Sam, I'm right out of dead rats," I quipped back.

"Them's everywhere," he replied darkly. "Never more than a few yards away from a rat. They'll be eating them windfalls in yon orchard no doubt."

I shuddered. "Too much information Sam."

"When you lives in the country…" his voice trailed off.

I looked into his eyes for that glint that that normally telegraphed his black humour but I was left unsure. His face did brighten considerably though when I reached for my wallet and paid him handsomely for his week-end labours.

I spent the best part of Wednesday and Thursday mornings raking up apples in my orchard and transferring the piles into the large paper sacks that I had bought in Hereford. My aches and pains had worn off and I felt a surge of energy from re-invigorated muscles. Perhaps I was meant for this country life after all. The intoxicating smell of rotting apples on a damp

Autumnal orchard floor seemed to be implanting itself into my psyche, one I would never forget. And the smell that built up in the fermenting room was of the same distinctive odour. By Thursday afternoon I counted thirty-two sacks of cider apples waiting to be transported to the mill – probably four car loads. That would not be practical. But first I needed to find a market for them. I telephoned Bulmers and was put through to the Fruit Office. Did I have a contract? The result was a polite but firm negative. I tried Westons in Much Marcle and received the same reply. I contacted several artisan makers and was passed from pillar to post, receiving one offer only, from a small outfit in the Brecon Beacons, where the costs of delivery would have outweighed any profit attainable. It would have meant my working at half the minimum wage and surrendering the apples for free. Perhaps I should have listened to Sam in the first place.

Peter telephoned intent in arranging a rendezvous in the Dog and Duck for that evening. I readily agreed, not expecting him to arrive at the pub with a shapely blonde glued to his arm. "Desmond, meet Nora. She's one of my best customers." For exactly what I dared not ask.

She was fair falling out of a leather jacket with skin tight leather trousers to match; obviously fighting the forties and just about holding her own in the process. Bright red lipstick encircling a warm smile, fingernails to match – all perfect – not a hair out of place, just like Peter. I had to admit that I felt blood rushing to parts of my anatomy that had become unaccustomed to such intrusion.

Peter ordered me a fresh pint and one for himself. Nora settled for a slimline soft drink. "Nora's driving," smirked Peter happily. "She's just bought a bright red Mercedes Sports from me and won't allow me behind the wheel."

"With lovely white leather seats," added the woman eagerly, "and goes like a bomb."

"And I bet you go like a train," I thought.

Clearly Peter wanted to dispense with the small talk and get to his purpose in arranging our rendezvous. He must have warned Nora beforehand because she exhibited no impatience at the focussed conversation that followed, but rather seemed content to remain an observer.

"I don't expect that you've heard of the WZRG, Des," started my companion. I nodded an confirmation. "Neither had I before now. That stands for the War Zone Recovery Group. They specialise in digging up downed WW2 planes – especially Allied aircraft. They're big and well funded and it just so happens that they have a team out in Basse Normandy as I speak." The excitement poured out of Peter's eyes. "Lieutenant Ricci's missing Mustang was on their 'To Find' list but they were out of clues as to where it might be. I have spoken to Simon Mellor, who's big in their organisation and he reckons, from what I have told him, that they may have a good idea as to the crash location."

"My word." I gulped in genuine amazement.

"And their group out there have had to abort a search they were planning to make and are free to divert to finding our Mustang. They want me to ask Ricci a couple of questions should he come through again this coming Sunday. Simon has asked if you would mind him being there, if and when the call comes through?"

I took a long swig of beer before answering. I had been delving into memories from my past whilst raking up apples in the orchard earlier in the week and then, quite unexpectedly, these came to some sort of fruition. "Have you ever meddled with the Ouija board, Peter?"

Puzzlement was evident on my companion's face. "No, so what?"

Nora added a "Nor me neither."

"I'll tell you. Years ago, twenty-five or more, Angela and I had friends round to our house and we had an improvised Ouija session much as a party game – light amusement. There was lots of laughing and joking and drinking but towards the end of the session the glass, each of us with a finger on it, started moving very positively. Of course we blamed each other for propelling it but even with only a couple of fingers on the glass it seemed to have developed a mind and momentum of its own – or something else's mind. We were hooked and that led to several more sessions and some startling results. The information that the board gave us was often not what we asked of it and I came to the conclusion that we were dredging up a succession of malevolent spirits, not just one. It was so spooky that Angela and I put a stop to the sessions forthwith."

"And your point is?" asked Peter in obvious confusion.

"The sessions took place in the dining room of our house built in the 1930's. Instead of a picture rail, a plate rail ran all round the room at the same height. Laugh at me as you might, I became convinced that the spirits we had dredged out of the Ouija board, instead of returning to the dark hell from where they had emanated, were effectively sitting on the plate rail waiting to do mischief."

"That is spooky," said Nora drawing in her bosom.

"Don't be absurd," said Peter confidently. "That's a load of bollocks."

"I would have said the same," I conceded, "and I am usually pretty level headed and unflappable. Bur from that day forward the dining room appeared to be always cold. Walking past its open door, even on a summer's day, and the coldness of the dining room was no trick of the imagination. Luckily my job transferred me elsewhere and we sold the house soon afterwards."

"Is that it?" said Peter dismissively.

"Not quite. A young couple with children bought the house – I remember the wife's excitement. I probably sold it too cheap and they had a bargain. But within three months she was dead; killed in a car accident."

"Pure coincidence." Peter retorted.

"I think that I can see where you're coming from," sympathised Nora with a tight smile, her red lips pressed hard together.

I remember thinking, "She's wearing that colour lipstick to co-ordinate with her new sports car."

"You're linking your Ouija board experience with the spirit coming through the telephone, Des?" As usual, Peter was quick on the uptake. "How do we get round that one?"

My thought processes had not gotten that far so I was surprised in hearing myself reply, "Come and collect the telephone from me on Saturday morning and you can entertain this Simon bloke to a private hearing in your flat. Raking those apples allowed me time to think. I am worried that the telephone is another form of Ouija board; a different catalyst for evil spirits. I don't want to take any chances. Call me a wimp if you like. "

There was a period of silence broken by the statement from Peter, "but it might not work in my pad."

"That or nothing," I responded flatly. "That or nothing. And we keep this party between ourselves."

CHAPTER FIVE

Peter turned up at Well Cottage as I had expected he would, and took the telephone away with him. "Good riddance," I mouthed as Peter's car swung out of my drive. My outburst was aimed at the instrument of course, not at Peter.

I didn't hear from him again until halfway through December. Neither did I telephone him to enquire whether there had been further Saturday night encounters with Lieutenant Ricci because I felt that I had somewhat disgraced myself by abdicating from the centre of action, so to speak. And there were no meetings in the Dog and Duck because, I liked to think, Peter had more pressing business in the arms of the gorgeous Nora.

I certainly did not miss having the French telephone sitting on my dresser. I wouldn't have minded if I never saw the darned thing ever again. I know that Sam was of the same mind although, strangely, he never brought the subject into our conversation. I often tried to imagine him as a much younger man spending lonely nights guarding his sheep on the Welsh hills. Not that they were his sheep; he had never had more than a few pennies to rub together during the whole of his life. I wondered if he shared his toil with a sheepdog – or two even. How the world has changed.

Sam was in his element in nurturing the fermenting cider in the garage cum fermenting room. I was glad that the beverage was receiving the best attention – probably the very best. I did not entirely trust him not to have had a dead rat or two stashed away in his weather worn raincoat but – what the heck?

One evening, when Sam had had a gut full of cider and was starting to click his tongue and wheeze as was his wont, he threw his flat cap onto the kitchen floor next to Denzil who was innocently playing with his favourite silver bottle top. "Do you think that this ere kitty could lift up my cap?" Just for good measure, Sam slipped off the obnoxious headgear and half threw it over the cat – completely engulfing and imprisoning the poor animal.

I didn't know whether to be more concerned for Denzil's plight or relent to the fascination of Sam's bald pate its whiteness in contrast the berry leathery brown of the rest of his face. Did he wear the filthy thing in bed? "Come off it Sam, of course he can't."

"Ee can y'know. Corse ee can."

Sam was never a betting man so I knew that a wager wasn't in the offing. What was the old bugger up to? "O.K. Sam, you win, show me how."

Sam lifted the cap from off the bewildered kitten and dropped it down again beside Denzil. The poor mite looked round and then up at me as though to say "Why didn't you come to my rescue Dad?" I felt an obligatory pang of remorse. With a snap of his fingers Sam reached down and caught the kitten by his tail, lifted him into the air and dangled him over the offensive headgear. Denzil's claws sprung out automatically and grabbed at the only object close to him. Sam lifted the kitten higher and up came Denzil, cap and all.

I was suitably horrified. That particular incident would be seared into my memory bank for ever and a day, no doubt about that. I thought that Denzil would never forgive me – but the little chap did eventually.

One early evening, after Sam had gone on his way, I received a call from Peter. "Sorry, long time no see. I've been rather busy."

"With work or Nora?"

"Both I'm glad to say. She's some woman – very demanding though."

"How's that?"

"Wouldn't you like to know – but I'm not going to tell you."

That could mean anything. I let it pass. "Got any further with finding the airplane?"

"Yes, heaps. Simon's WZRG people have located the crash site much where the pilot says he came down. There's a circle of trees close to the straight road the pilot talked about. He must have just veered off as he was coming in to land on the road. In the centre is an old stone quarry, donkey's years old, which has long since filled up with water. Simon's people have taken some soundings – I don't understand the electronics involved – and they are certain that there is something worth investigating. They won't commit to saying that it's our aircraft but there's a definite smugness in the air – if you understand me."

"So where do they go from there?"

"They've contacted the farmer who owns the crash site and he has agreed to allow the Group to investigate further for a fee. He is after all a Normande – they don't usually miss a trick. And the pond needs draining first. It is a condition that the farmer does that – at a price. And then to supply the necessary digging machinery when the actual investigation starts."

"And when is that likely to happen?"

"Depends on the weather. But most of the WZRG are volunteers with ongoing work commitments. Between Christmas and New Year would leave enough of them free for a trip to France. And you're invited to come and watch as the Group's guest, being as if it wasn't for you the site probably wouldn't have been discovered. You'll be guest of honour and all that. I'm invited too of course. Actually, I'm considered to be one of the team."

"I'll certainly give that some thought…"

"We must have a beer sometime. Got to go."

Christmas was only a fortnight away and I had no idea as to how and where I would embrace the festivities. My daughter had married an Australian and was making merriment in Sydney, her adopted home, by all accounts. I did not like to be reminded that my son was currently a guest of Her Majesty serving his time in an open prison in Sussex with his fellow embezzlers. To say that we were estranged would have been a falsehood. Of course I was hung up over his lack of remorse for his victims but blood is blood after all. Thankfully his sins had come to light after Angela's death and she was spared the shame and humiliation of Tom's disgrace.

There was a second element that I had tried hard to learn to live with. I had enjoyed a lucrative position, one with some considerable authority in the City of London's financial district, and had used my influence to help get Tom's career launched. As a child Tom had always been bright, quick to focussed and as a very young man he took to the intricacies of finance like a duck to water. He made legitimate money, lots of it, but that wasn't enough. He wanted to be a financial mogul and he broke rules in his endeavour to achieve that objective.

Next evening I told Sam about my invitation as he quaffed, and I sipped cider. "Wild osses wouldn't get me to Frogland." No change there.

"Would you feed Denzil for me whilst I am away?"

"'Appen I would. Got to keep me eye on the cider anyway," he agreed grudgingly. Although I think he was quite pleased to know that I trusted him.

"That's sorted then," I said closing the subject.

"What you goin' to do with them apples in the paper sacks?"

I had not forgotten them but I wished that I could. "I dunno. Nobody seems to wants them. I've tried."

Sam pretended to think hard. "Ed Weston with give you a few quid for 'em – feeds 'em to his hogs."

"Ed Weston?"

"Pig farmer over Birham way."

"Would he really?"

"I could ask him if you want." The craftiness in Sam's offer was hard to miss. Whatever this Ed Weston was willing to pay would be halved by the time the price reached my ears. What the hell. I was so pissed off with cider apples I would probably be willing to give them away anyway.

"Do that please, Sam. That's kind of you."

The old shepherd tried hard to suppress a smirk of pure satisfaction.

True to form the stack of paper sacks disappeared in double quick time and Sam duly handed over a sum so paltry that he did not have the courage to allow his eyes to meet mine. I had a vision of Sam keeping cavey down the lane watching for me to leave the cottage – and then calling in his partner in crime, Ed Weston, when I did so.

A week before I was due to leave for France I started to have misgivings. These translated into a couple of sleepless nights. The obvious way forward seemed to be to discuss my reservations with Peter and I did manage to catch him by telephone early evening. He seemed genuinely please to hear from me.

"Hi Des, I was about to get in touch with you as it so happens. The French farmer has drained the pond and the excavation is to start on the twenty-seventh. If you want Christmas at home you'll need to travel over on the 27th. I don't think that Brittany Ferries operate on Boxing Day. I'm going over earlier with Nora and spending Christmas with Patrick and Joan of Arc." He tittered at his own joke. "Can't offer to take you, old lad, because we're going over in the Mercedes; two-seater. I didn't think that you'd want to stay with Patrick anyway."

"That's O.K. Peter, I can organise a hotel near the crash site, no problem. Where exactly is it?" Cowardly I had ducked my overnight resolution to distance myself from the project entirely.

"Two kilometres from the village of La Peneille, Basse Normandy. It's a bit tricky to find so I am told but I'll pop over with a map for you in the next few days. Sy's given me full directions."

So it was Sy now, not Simon; very chummy." I want to ask you about Simon and his WZKP. How kosher are they?"

"Kosher?"

"Yeh. Are they a recognised group of aviation archaeologists?"

"Aviation archaeologists? That's a new one on me."

"Well, it strikes me that these crash sites are of historical importance and, if things are as they appear, our one is a war grave. Is it alright for people to go digging them up willy-nilly?"

I could hear Peter take a large intake of breath. "I suppose, if they were to find remains of pilot Ricci then the relevant authorities will have to be informed."

"And who might they be?"

Again there was a delay in replying. "The American embassy I guess."

"Not the French authorities?"

"Them as well if those are the rules. Look, I can see where you're coming from Des, but I don't have the answers. I will need talk to Sy Mellor and come back to you. I am sure he's got all the angles well sorted."

"If this bloke Sy, as you now call him, has all the paperwork in place then I'm right behind the project but if he's the head of a gang of trophy hunters I want nothing more to do with this."

"I get you Des. Keep your hair on – not that there's much left of it. Give me twenty-four hours…"

True to his word Peter came back to me about the same time the following day. "Everything's above board, Des. I have spoken to Simon and he assures me that the French farmer – him what owns the land – has approached the Maire of Peneille and has permission to excavate the site. Power is devolved downwards in France and local Maires have considerable authority. You probably know that already?"

"Yes." I agreed.

"I am also assured that the first sign of any human remains will be reported to the Maire immediately and through him the authorities in Paris and America and, whoever else, will be notified."

"He didn't say that the digging would stop immediately in such a eventuality?"

"No. He didn't say that. But they will take great care in how they proceed. There is a big investment in time and effort, let alone cost, in setting up and conducting the operation. These boys are mainly only part-timers remember and the organisation has limited funds."

"How is the WZRG funded?" I asked.

Peter sighed audibly. "I didn't ask. I can't think of everything."

I might have been mollified on another day and a different sequence of events – or even after a decent night's sleep. Instead I woke the next morning with an unpleasant taste in my mouth, both actually and metaphorically. I fed Denzil and then played with him for a while. He scooted round the kitchen floor chasing the inevitable bottle top which made me chuckle. He eclipsed any tonic that could be found in a pill box or a bottle. Finally, with him snoozing on my lap I allowed my mind to wander. How could I get information about the WZRG?

I hadn't a computer as in those days few people had heard of Google – even if the website existed then. There was always the library of course but, it being Saturday, I felt disinclined to drive into Hereford and join the struggle through the traffic there. The Town Planning Department had been playing with the idea of a by-pass for decades. It took a while for me to come round to the idea of the American War Museum at Duxford, Peter's font of all knowledge. Now, what was the name of the researcher he had befriended? A minor miracle considering the state of my memory, yet the name came to me – Janice Farmer.

I used the online directory to obtain the Museum's number and, as luck would have it, Janice Farmer was on duty that morning. I hadn't expected to talk to her in person as Peter had given me the impression that she was a part-time volunteer and there in post on some week-days. I was delighted and introduced myself using Peter Brody's name as a point of reference. The car salesman had left an impression on her and that further oiled the machinery of communication. What did she know of the WZRG?

"Are they involved in the case of the Mustang that Mr. Brody's been enquiring about?" she answered my question with one of her own with a unmistakeable tone of suspicion..

"Is that of concern to you?" I said, not answering her question directly either. Two could play at that game.

"It could well be of concern Mr. Harper."

"Can we share information, perhaps?"

"I'm loath to discuss this over the phone with a stranger."

"Quite proper of you. I fully understand. But believe you me we are singing from the same hymn sheet. And you're a stranger to me as well."

"But you know who I am and where I am. Who are you and where are you, Mr. Harper?"

I answered her questions and added, without giving details, that there was a possible crash site in France about to be excavated by the WZRG.

"If you are in any way connected to the WZRG or are in contact with them you must warn them to desist from any excavation unless they have full and complete paperwork and authority to do so. I know that they haven't permission from the American Authorities and I very much doubt that they have from the French who are very strict about war memorials – as they classify and monitor them."

"You've obviously had dealings with the WZBG before?"

"Oh constantly." She let slip the disgust in her voice. I tried pushing her and I thought for a moment that I had broken through. "I know the law in this country that appertains to slander, Mr. Harper and for all I know you could be a fully paid up member of the WZRG. Even if you are just a bystander all I will say is something that is in the Public Domain i.e. is common knowledge. There is a shop in Birmingham with a big postal trade, especially in exports to the USA, selling war relics. Companies House lists one of its directors to be a Mr. Simon Delaney Mellor."

"Thank you Mrs. Farmer. Thank you very much," I breathed into the phone.

"It's Miss actually."

"Thank you kindly Miss Farmer."

I rang Peter straight away and wasn't surprised to be diverted to his answer phone. I left a simple message asking him to ring me; no details. I fretted the rest of the day waiting for his call.

When Sam's time grew imminent I put off all the lights and pretended that the house was empty. I heard him grumbling off towards the Dog and Duck after he had unsuccessfully tried the door several times. Denzil had meowed at him, probably trying to tell him that I was in hiding. Stupid cat.

Peter appeared unexpectedly in person as noon was nigh on that Sunday. He looked well – sleek even. Obviously the ministrations of the lovely Nora were having a beneficial effect on him. We small talked as I made coffee, hardly containing myself not to spill my news. At last the time came.

"I spoke with Miss Farmer at Duxford yesterday."

"Oh," exclaimed Peter, wide eyed. "Janice – did she tell you what you wanted?"

"I've serious concerns about the digging up of the remains of the Mustang."

"I realise that," said Peter soothingly, "but there's no need, Des. Everything is under control and out of your hands."

"The point is what the Recovery Group is doing is illegal."

"Illegal? How come?"

"They need permissions in writing. From the French Government certainly and the Americans too most likely. This is a potential war grave that is about to be violated."

"We don't know that for sure. I have already told you that if we find any sign of the pilot the digging will stop. I have spoken to Simon about it and he has assured me again that will be the outcome. As he says, every time you find bits and pieces of war zone paraphernalia, debris that is, you can't go running off to the authorities. They would be overwhelmed with notifications with things as innocuous as bits of shrapnel and shell cases. They don't expect that."

"So what's Simon Mellor's angle in all this, Peter?"

"He's a historian, an enthusiast, er, er, an aviation archaeologist to use your description."

"Bollocks."

"You what?"

"It's bollocks. He's a director of a limited company in Birmingham selling war memorabilia and much of it is ending up in the USA."

"Did the Farmer woman tell you that?"

"Yes."

Peter was clearly shaken. I gave him time for the news to sink in and make an impression. He slurped his coffee by way of a diversion. Eventually he asked, "What, if anything, do you intend to do with that information?"

"I'm not going to France for a start,"

"No, no, of course not," murmured Peter, his brain obviously racing. "But… are you going to alert the authorities?"

"What authorities? I wouldn't know where to start. And if I did and the excavation turned out to be a bum steer, I would end up as a laughing stock – especially if I mention the telephone calls on a dilapidated pre-war French instrument that is not even connected to the system."

"You've given the matter some thought, Des." We talked for about half an hour, the main focus being the expedition to France and what might be found as a result of the excavation. Finally Peter stood up and making himself ready to depart, "I've decided – I'm going through with this. I have promised Nora a romantic week-end and she would be really disappointed if I pull out now. Patrick too. If we do find something significant from the dig at least I will be there with a chance to reign the WZRG in and persuade them to do the right thing. I'll take it upon myself to make sure they won't have carte blanche to dispose of artefacts illegitimately, if that is indeed what they're up to."

To me that sounded realistic and I effectively gave Peter my blessing enabling us to part in good humour. I did feel a twang of disappointment at having dropped out but I was convinced that I had made the correct decision.

I received an unexpected invitation to spend Christmas with ex-neighbours, Phil and Patricia, in Harlow and I grabbed the opportunity. Anything had to be better than a lonely Christmas Day and Boxing Day in Well Cottage. I already had Sam geared up to look after Denzil and he did not mind the change in the dates. I also contacted Springside Open Prison in Sussex and booked a visit to my son, Tom, on the 27th.

There was enough time left that Saturday afternoon for me to venture into Hereford and buy Christmas presents for my Harlow hosts. What could I get for Sam Williams? I alighted on a Harris Tweed flat cap and a scarf to match. For Denzil I found three small balls with a jingle mechanism inside. He could chase them round the kitchen floor to his wee heart's content. I was unsure of the prison rules as regards Tom and eventually settled on a couple of books; one of crosswords and the other Sudoku. He was, after all, proven to be brilliant at words and figures; too clever for his own good many would say.

Spending Christmas in Harlow turned out to be a very good idea indeed. Phil and Patricia were brilliant hosts and their extended family embraced me. On Boxing Day we went off to Newmarket Races and I won a pot of money on a couple of outsiders. I am not a betting man, because I don't like losing, but modest stakes on two long-odds nags brought a return that paid for the drinks and food for all our party. That pleased me no end.

On the drive down to Sussex the heavens opened and continued to do so for most of that day. My thoughts frequently wandered to that wood in Normandy, wondering whether they were in receipt of the same extreme weather. If so would that put a temporary halt to the excavations there?

I was used to Tom being in denial about the justice in his prison sentence. He had championed his innocence from the moment he found police officers knocking on the front door of his luxury Thames-side flat – penthouse no less. The jury at the Old Bailey were not taken in by his voluminous protests but, in my opinion, the judge was lenient. He was assessed in a high security prison but soon transferred to a Category D Open Prison – Springside, in Sussex which my son cheerfully likened to a holiday camp.

At the reception desk a female officer with a huge bosom and easy smile checked me in. "So, you've come to see Tom Harper. Are you his father? We all know prisoner Harper. Nice chap but can he talk? Rabbit, rabbit, rabbit." Her male companion went through the motions of frisking me, ensuring that I had not cut out the insides of the two quiz books in order to conceal contraband.

Tom was full of ideas as to how he was going to make an even bigger fortune come his release. Whilst I was pleased that he was not wallowing in fits of depression or engaging in thoughts of self-harm, I was concerned that he could be heading for another incarceration and a much longer sentence. I chose to remind him that he was blackballed as far as the City of London was concerned and prohibited by Companies House to hold the office of company director for five years.

"Don't concern yourself about that, Dad," he responded cheerfully. "There's all manner of ways of getting round such trivial obstacles. Besides, the City is just a geographical blob when you compare it to the whole world. I've got contacts in India, Mexico City and several offshore havens. The world will be my proverbial oyster when I can get free from here. There's some clever guys in this place. We've been getting together and…"

"Don't tell me son. Just don't tell me." Even so I had to admire his fortitude – silently of course.

I was home too late that day to catch Sam. All seemed well as I arrived at the cottage and Denzil was appropriately pleased to see me and was none the worse for having been subject to Sam's brief patronage. I was also pleased to see that he had evidently gotten the hang of the cat flap that I had had installed for him in the kitchen door. I reminded myself that I needed to take him to the vet to be checked over, vaccinated and chipped. How remiss of me.

The next day I glimpsed Sam walking past the kitchen door heading, I supposed, for the fermenting room. I did not chase after him – he would have known that I was home because of the car in the drive. I was playing with Denzil and one of his tingle balls when Sam did eventually chap the door and walk in. He was carrying a five gallon white plastic container which I did not recognise. It was transparent enough to indicate a yellowish liquid – either cider or urine… Of course, it could be cider that tasted like "piss" – to quote Sam.

The old shepherd plonked the container on the kitchen table and stood back to watch my reaction. I could tell that he was proud of the contents because his usual greeting to me, a touch to the peak of his cap, a hint of a smile and "yers alright?" had been dispensed with. I played the same game. "What's that in there Sam? Piss?"

"Best piss you'll git to taste, Gaffer."

"Go on," I said reaching for two glasses. Sam filled both with an obvious pride judging by the look on his weather-beaten and gnarled face. For still cider it was somewhat lively and appetising. I smelled first and then took a tentative sip. That turned quickly into several mouthfuls. "My goodness Sam, that tastes bloody good."

If the old man had had a tail he would have wagged it wildly. He was unbelievably pleased with my approbation. He lost ten years or a hundredweight sack from off his shoulders in a trice. "Aye", he agreed, "that be a good drop of juice."

I needed a refill and then another. Sam matched me. Then a thought struck me. "Do I detect a slight touch of whisky in the background? This has come out of one of those whisky barrels hasn't it?"

Sam's face fell slightly. He did not want to admit that this fine cider was not entirely as a result of his cider making prowess. But there could be no denying that the whisky barrel had added an unusual and beneficial ingredient to the process. "Appen it's not done any 'arm."

I gave Sam his Christmas presents. He made me feel bad by apologising for not having one for me. I didn't mean to embarrass the old boy. Cautiously he pulled the scarf from out of its colourful paper and held the garment up along its length. "That's just the job, Gaffer, keep me old throat warm, that will." He moved on to the second parcel. The cap was an entirely different proposition. I could tell that at once with a vision of Sam walking into the Tap Room where the old codgers congregated. They would no doubt take the Michael out of his new "bonnet" mercilessly. Sam struggled for an appropriate comment. "I'll keep that for Sunday best," was the best that he could come up with. He would probably wear it one day but only after it had been kicked right round a shitty cow byre.

New Year's Eve arrived and I still had not received a word from Peter. I had tried his mobile phone many times but it had not rung let alone been answered. I alternated between irritation at being so ignored and concern that he might be in trouble of some sort. If he were locked up in a French jail he would not have the means to contact me. I did think of ringing

Patrick but I could not find his number – not that I tried very hard to locate it.

I did my 'lights off' trick at teatime to thwart Sam. I remember thinking that I would not get away with that in the Spring and the lighter evenings. I would have to think of a different Machiavellian practice. I had decided to pop down to the Dog and Duck for an hour or two but not to see in the New Year. At least there would be some lively company. I had just imprisoned Denzil in the kitchen prior to my departure when I heard a car scrunching into the cottage's forecourt.

CHAPTER SIX

As soon as I opened the front door I recognised the car. I could hardly have failed to do so; a bright red Mercedes Sports. Yet I needed to confirm from its number plate that it was indeed the spotless machine as I had last seen it. Dried mud was splattered everywhere and that meant not just up the sides from off road driving but across the hard top, boot and bonnet. I could not tell for sure but it looked as though it had suffered more permanent damage; not localised as from an accident but bits and pieces all over.

The driver had not hurried to make an exit so I could not tell whether the car was occupied by Nora or Peter or both of them. I soon solved that uncertainty by walking up the driver's side to find Nora alone. But not the glamorous Nora whom I had so admired and who had set my pulse racing; no make-up, puffy bloodshot eyes, a woman obviously in some serious distress.

"Good God, Nora, you look dreadful." Not exactly a reaction I was to be proud of, as I reflected later. "Come inside and I'll make you a cup of tea." A good old British failsafe; just as banal. I led her into the kitchen, sat her down at the table and activated the electric kettle. Denzil, perceiving a new playmate and admirer started meowing and rubbing himself against her legs. I picked him up rather too roughly and put him outside, switching the cat flap to be non-operable. Nora was silent as I mashed the tea, put two cups on the table and sat down to join her.

I had contained the question on the tip of my tongue as long as I could. "Where's Peter?"

"Peter's dead," she said simply and then broke down into floods of tears. I fetched a box of tissues from the dresser, resumed my seat and waited patiently. My instinct had been to put my arms round her but I fell short of the confidence to do that. To my way of thinking she had obviously come to tell me what had happened in France. All I needed to do was give her the time, space and empathy.

"We were so happy driving down through France to Patrick's place. I was warned about his wife but she could not have been nicer and we had a super Christmas. On Boxing Day Pete proposed to me…" That revelation brought on a fresh bout of tears. "We had only known each other for a month or so, six fantastic weeks. I told him to wait and ask me again at Easter." More paper tissues were required.

"Next day we set off early to meet with the people from the Recovery Group. There were six of them, the farmer and his son and us two, ten in all. This bloke Simon was giving the orders and seemed to be hurrying the job along."

"What was the place like?" I interrupted. "The topography?" I added for want of a better word.

"We found the Recovery Groups vehicles parked on the roadside next to a huge ploughed field. Peter explained to me that there used to be small fields with lots of hedgerows but to accommodate modern tractors and equipment the hedges had been grubbed up. There was a big clump of trees on one side of the field, some way off from the road. We had to walk over the ploughed field to get to it." Another bout of tears interrupted her story. "Amongst the trees was a dried up pond. Peter said that the farmer had emptied out all the water just days before we arrived."

"Peter told me about that.".

"Walking across the muddy field to the trees the ground was all churned up from the farmer's digger. My boots were like doughnuts."

"I get the picture." I smiled encouragingly.

"When we got to the trees, the farmer's son was operating the digger. One like you see over here. A JCB type thing. He had already dug out one edge of the pond so as he could get his machine low enough to dig out the pond bottom, if that makes sense to you. He was then pulling out soil or whatever from the bottom of the pond, swinging the grab round and depositing the earth to both sides. The farmer and Simon and five other WZRG guys were watching."

"Was it raining?" I asked, mindful of the weather when I had driven down to Sussex.

"No. It had done, that's why the field was so wet and muddy."

"Go on, Nora."

"After a short while a wheel, or the remains of a wheel, appeared. It was upright before the bucket on the digger knocked it over. At that point the digger was ordered out of the pond and the WZ men went down into the hole to investigate. They poked around with spades and trowels and things for ages. In the end they agreed that the wheel probably belonged to a Mustang and that the plane was upside down in the ground. Peter was ecstatic – so excited."

"I can understand that," I said, an image of the French telephone flashing across my brain.

"Peter saw the farmer's son changing the bucket on the digger for a smaller one and realised that the Group had little intention of halting the digging. He told Simon they needed to stop there – that the site was almost certainly classed as a war grave. Peter went on about them breaking the law and if the remains of the pilot were inside the cockpit he might still have relatives in America and – and stuff like that. Things became heated between them and the others of the Recovery Group joined in, all of them against Peter. Simon then signalled to the farmer and he apparently told his son to get back into the hole with the digger and carry on."

Nora's tears had dried up and now she was fully focussed in telling her story. "Peter told me to go to the car and fetch his mobile which was in the glove compartment. He said to check for a signal and if it were nil or low he said I should drive off to the nearest police station and get help. Otherwise I was to take the phone back to him and he would contact the Gendarmerie. As I was sitting in the car reaching for the mobile I saw two of the Research Group and the farmer heading for me. I was very scared indeed. I was saved by the biggest bang that I have ever heard in my life.. Stuff rained down all around and over the car; stones, branches, clumps of things. It was horrendous and has ruined my poor car. Not that that matters in the compared to Peter's death."

That thought was enough to set her off again and I handed out more tissues. This time I caught her hand and gave it an encouraging squeeze. "Peter, the farmer's son, and two Recovery Group men were killed outright. Simon Mellor is very seriously injured and has lost both legs. I am the only one to come out of it unscathed, apart from the two recovery people and the farmer who were chasing after me. Physically unscathed that is – mentally I am a total mess."

I encouraged Nora to take another sip of tea. "After the explosion what happened then?"

"I was so shocked I couldn't think of what to do. The mobile phone did have a signal but I hadn't a clue what the French equivalent of 999 was. But one of the WZ men had enough of his wits left to take over and he got through to… whoever. I don't know. The police came in dribs and drabs. I suppose they are thin on the ground in rural Normandy. I was arrested and taken to a Gendarmerie in a town whose name I cannot remember or pronounce. It's written on paperwork that I brought home with me."

"You were arrested?" I asked.

"Yes, and held for two days in a police cell. Evidently the Group had broken all manner of laws just as poor Peter had warned them."

"Have the police charged you personally with any offence, Nora?"

"No, I told the whole truth and I think that they believed my story. I was given access to a lawyer and she confirmed that I was free to go but that I could still be called back and prosecuted should conflicting information come to light – or something like that."

"And your car was drivable obviously?"

"Yes, just roadworthy. I shall put in an insurance claim and if it is not written off I shall get rid of it. It's because of the car that I met Peter. He sold it to me. It's all so sad. To think that Peter asked me to marry him only the day before he died."

We talked on and when the time came I offered to drive Nora home to her flat. Surprisingly she agreed and I took her in my car. She said that she would arrange to retrieve her Mercedes in a day or so. I did manage to remember to let an annoyed Denzil back into the kitchen and reset the cap flap to 'fully operational' mode.

In my car on the way to her flat Nora confided in me further. "I hate those WZRG people."

I remember thinking that she had remembered the group's full acronym. "Why particularly?"

"When I was in the Gendarmerie I was left in a room with one of them; the bloke who helped me and summoned the police after the explosion. He said that it was all Peter's fault. I thought that he meant because Peter had listened to the telephone calls and everything that happened started from there."

"That sounds likely," I agreed.

"But that wasn't what he was on about. Evidently Peter told Simon Mellor that the Mustang had been loaded with rockets and machine gun rounds – that it was on a mission to shoot up trains and military convoys. Nothing was said about a great big bomb. Someone in the Gendarmerie said it was five hundred kilograms most likely. If the Group had known that, they would have approached the excavation in an entirely different way."

"I know that the researchers at the American War Museum told Peter about the light ammunition. There never was mention of a bomb – not to my knowledge anyway."

"Then the museum people have something to answer for. It wasn't Peter's fault."

Nora had a point there. She thanked me for my kindness and disappeared into a block of flats, slouching pathetically away.

Sam took the news of Peter's death with his normal stoicism; nothing more than a grunt and a hand rubbed across his stubbly chin. I was obliged to remember that he had dealt with death on a daily basis on those bleak hills of his. The sheep in his flock were his children. Yet he did relapse into a silence which I would have liked to think was in deference to our fallen comrade.

I happened to travel the Worcester Road out of Hereford the following day and passing Rillington's Garage. I could hardly fail to notice the flag on their leading pole – the union flag – was flying at half mast. That brought a lump in my throat and thoughts about Peter's funeral. I hadn't asked Nora; probably just as well. I chided myself for wondering if Peter had been blown to smithereens and if there was anything left of him that would warrant a burial or a cremation. Poor bastard.

The damaged red car stayed on my frontage for nearly a week and I began to wonder if Nora was still functioning. I had visions of her having harmed herself such was her grief, or having retreated into a deep depression. I had no means of contacting her without knocking on doors in the block of flats that I had seen her disappear into. The only link between us had been Peter. I even telephoned Rillington's Garage to see if they could help – but they had no contact details either.

The longer that bruised red sports car stood outside my lounge window the more I whittled about the misinformation that Peter had received from the Duxford people. Peter had been told that Ricci's Mustang had been lightly armed and that falsehood had cost him his life. I just could not let that conundrum rest unsolved and that translated into talking to Miss Janice Farmer. I was obliged to make six telephone calls over three days before I managed to track her down.

She remembered me all too well and knew about the disaster at Peneille. "This is what happens when people like you break the rules. I regret the loss of life but you have only yourselves to blame."

"Hang fire one minute Miss Farmer," I countered tersely. "I fully registered what you told me and I dropped out from going to watch the excavation. You possibly saved my life." I had worked out that angle before making the telephone calls to Duxford as a deliberate ploy to get their co-operation. "And I told my friend Peter what you told me and I know that he tried to persuade the WZRG to abort the enterprise pending official permission. When they uncovered the first sign of the aircraft Peter tried to stop the dig to the extent of sending off his lady friend to ring the local police. That saved her life by the way."

"Oh, if that's true I didn't realise," said the voice somewhat repentantly. "Then I can understand how upset you are. I'm sorry."

"The thing is, Miss Farmer, Peter contacted yourselves some time ago and part of the information he was given was that Lieutenant Ricci's Mustang was only lightly armed. His mission evidently was to disrupt German movements prior to D-Day. The authorities in France, I am told, reckon that the plane was buried with an unexploded five hundred kilogram bomb."

"Do you know who he spoke to here at Duxford?"

"No. He didn't say – or if he did I don't remember."

"Well, we don't keep a record normally of the information that we give out, but I'll make some enquiries and ring you back, Mr. Harper."

"You assure me that you will?"

"Absolutely."

Janice Farmer was as good as her word but the wait was a long one with me getting increasingly agitated as the hours slipped by. I was part way through feeding Denzil when my telephone burst into life and I left the kitten meowing in frustration as his supper was abandoned on the dresser undelivered.

"You must appreciate Mr. Harper, that we have a team of part-time volunteers here and if I were to ask every one of them it could take weeks if not months. But I have taken a comprehensive look at the flights recorded from Nosterham in Kent two weeks either side of the 4th June 1944. There were no operations in that part of Normandy focused on attacking German transport movements. The allies did not want to warn the enemy that an invasion was imminent. A few days before D-Day they did operate in the area attacking selected ground batteries in preparation for the gliders that were in the vanguard of the invasion."

"Are you absolutely sure that's true?"

"Lieutenant Ricci's orders for the fourth of June are clearly recorded. I am sure that none of our researchers could be left in any doubt. His Mustang was loaded with a thousand pound bomb and he was ordered to target a villa on the outskirts of Avranches in the Department of Manche – not all that far away from where he crashed. High Command in the U.K. had intelligence that there was a meeting of high ranking German military personnel at the villa and their permanent removal from that particular theatre of war would have been highly beneficial. Flight Lieutenant Ricci's mission was recorded as unsuccessful and, of course, that he failed to return to base."

"So how do you think Peter learned of his version of events?"

"Goodness knows. Dare I ask if he could have made it up for some reason of his own?"

That was a conundrum that would exercise my mind for many weeks to follow. I just couldn't imagine Peter to be that Machiavellian. He may have left his morals at home when he donned the role of car salesman but that was part of the job description. He had been nothing but straightforward with me as far as I was aware. If I were pushed into a corner to give an explanation I would not rule out the Ouija board syndrome.

I remembered imagining those spirits sitting malevolently on the plate rail of our home in Southend. The voice on the French telephone, purporting to be Flight Lieutenant Jaman K. Ricci was that of a spirit – no doubt about that. Was it really his voice I had heard? Or was it a ghostly imposter, bent on mischief? Only some months later was I informed by a sympathetic Janice Farmer that relics of the pilot had been identified amongst the debris at Peneille. Had false information somehow been conveyed to Peter? Could a spirit have somehow passed off as a researcher at Duxford? Questions, questions, questions – never to be answered.

Ten days after Nora's visit I came home from a shopping trip to a Hereford supermarket to find an empty space where the red car had stood. Waiting for me against the front door lay a plastic carrier bag with a note flapping in the wind, stapled to its topside. I rudely snatched off the paper and read what was written.

> *Dear Desmond,*
> *I should have come sooner but I haven't wanted to see anybody. I am going away to spend some time with my sister and her husband. I wanted to throw the enclosed from off the highest mountain or into the deepest sea. But as it belongs to you I will give you that pleasure.*
> *Nora. XX*

I did not need to open the bag to see what was contained inside. I left my shopping on the gravel, grabbed the carrier and took it down the garden to the rubbish corner, overgrown with briars and nettles, and threw it into the heart of the foliage, never to be disturbed as long as I was the owner of Well Cottage.

CHAPTER SEVEN

Lonely? Of course I was lonely at times. That was an affliction that I had suffered intermittently since Angela's untimely death.

Moving from Essex to Well Cottage had effectively isolated me from friendships built over many years. I did spent Christmas with Phil and Patricia in Harlow and other friends telephoned me on impulse, as I did them. My village, a dormitory for Hereford City and beyond, was full of housewives on week-days and countless couples in the various stages of retirement. Added to that my cottage was set apart from the village and so I was not in the centre of the little activity that was available.

That was shared between the village hall, shop, church and the Dog and Duck. By adopting the pub as regular refuge I feared that I would find myself increasingly being associated with the flies who sat at the bar on stools in a phalanx, obstructing access to the main body of customers. Additionally, the level of conversation of the stool occupiers was pretty banal. The other option was to occupy a table, preferably in a corner, with a sign over my head reading "lonely old man". I did not even consider joining the old ciderhead codgers in the Tap Room in the unlikely event that they would have accepted me. How I missed Peter...

I did consider a Singles Night in a Leominster Hotel that was regularly advertised in the weekly *Hereford Times* and I even got as far as the brightly lit entrance porch on one occasion before bottling out. How my life could have been different had I found the courage to take those final few steps. I yearned at times for female company but images of Angela somehow held me back.

I managed to convince Sam that his rights of passage through my kitchen door were restricted to Fridays, Saturdays and possibly Sundays, and only then if he found the door to be unlocked. I did not rule out special occasions though. If I allowed him he would be at my table seven days out of seven and I had not yet descended to that degree of loneliness.

Sam's stewardship of our cider making enterprise had not been a total success. The contents of one of the four whisky barrels had turned sour – "to vinegar" in Sam's words. Not the sort of vinegar that could be the base for a vinaigrette or sprayed over a fish supper? Apparently not. Sam sealed the offending barrel and unceremoniously rolled it out into the orchard and released its contents into the ground. "Back where it come from," he grunted watching the contents gulping out into the sward. He then utilised my garden hose and sprayed the inside assiduously. I was despatched to the home brew shop in Hereford to buy some "carbonate". The poor shopkeeper was at a loss to capture Sam's meaning until I explained the job at hand. Back in the garage, or fermenting room, the barrel then full of water laced with the chemical, was left to stand for a week and more.

We had been drinking "Well Cottage Cider" since before Christmas and the tapped barrel was less than half full. In addition there were two full barrels and much of the six plastic casks remaining in what was the Fermenting Room and had now become the Cider Store; fermentation having long ceased. "We needs to rack them buggers," said Sam.

"Rack?" I queried.

"Git a plastic bucket – two would be best." I obliged and Sam cleaned them out thoroughly although I thought them to be pretty nigh clean in the first place. "Got any thin rubber pipe?" I shook my head.. "Cut me a good couple of yards off the garden hose," ordered my companion.

"This job's not a good 'un" I moaned. Nevertheless I did his bidding.

Sam cleared an area on the work bench and I helped to lift the part full barrel into the space. Using the piece of hose he siphoned the good cider from out of the barrel into the buckets place d on the floor below. Their capacity no way equalled that of the barrel. Sam should have worked that out before embarking on the job. Luckily I had inherited an old tin bath from the previous owners and it was left to me to scrub it clean so that the remainder of the barrel could be siphoned therein. That was until the first signs of sediment appeared when the process was abruptly curtailed.

We rolled the barrel out into the garden and swilled out the sediment inside until Sam was entirely satisfied there was none left. I expected we would start laborious chore of ladling the cider languishing in the buckets and bath back to where it had come. But no, Sam had a better idea. He siphoned the cider from the second full cask into the newly empty one, watched for the sediment and then the process of cleaning was repeated. Similarly the third full barrel was decanted into the empty one and then cleaned. The cider in the buckets and bath we transferred into the cleaned third barrel. Job done.

No, not done. We needed to repeat the same process with the plastic kegs.

My euphoria on completion of such an arduous task was quickly evaporated when Sam announced, "They won't do much good in 'ere come Whitsuntide."

"What do you mean Sam?"

"Tin roof," answered Sam rolling his eyes upwards. "Be like an oven in 'ere."

"Oh." True enough, the roof of the garage was constructed of corrugated iron, 1930s vintage at a guess. "So, what's the answer to that?"

"Needs somewhere cool," answered Sam bluntly.

I didn't have to deliberate for long. "There's only the cellar."

I could hardly not notice the conflict that showed across Sam's weather-beaten face. "I don't likes it down there," he grumbled.

"There's nowhere else," I said emphatically.

And so it transpired that by the end of February three casks were chocked up and five plastic casks stood resplendent in Well Cottage's cool, dry cellar. There was electric light down there, the ceiling was high enough for me to stand upright, let alone Sam's diminutive five foot six inches, and the air remained fresh thanks to strategically placed airbricks in the front wall.

Interestingly Sam was not the only one with a dislike of my subterranean store. Denzil would normally be close at my heels as I conducted my chores around the cottage; that is when he wasn't curled up asleep in front of the Aga in the kitchen. The exception was he never followed me on my infrequent excursions down into the nether region of Well Cottage. When, on one occasion, I innocently took him down the stone steps with me he squirmed in my arms with such violence that I could not hold on to him. He gained the floor and scampered up the stairs as if his life depended on it. From then on, if I made for the cellar door he made a point of heading off in an opposite direction.

Time ticked by. March blew in cold and snowy and for a couple of days I was imprisoned; the lane into the village had become impassable. I remember that incident well because I received a very surprising telephone call from my son Tom. He was in high spirits having been told that he had been granted early release from his incarceration in Springside Prison in Sussex. "I've been a good boy," my exuberant son confided, "so I expected an early release date – but not quite so soon. It's to do with overcrowding I reckon. They need my bed…"

"When?" I asked.

"Any day now. They never tell you what's going on. Suspense seems to be part of the punishment. The thing is Dad…"

"Yes?"

"Can I come and live with you for a while?"

What could I say other than "Of course you can"? Yet such a request was completely out of character. Tom had been brilliant at school, especially in mathematics and languages, and had been pushed by his tutors to apply for Oxbridge. But nothing that Angela or I could say, or do, could persuade him not to leave school after his "A" levels. He was hell bent on a job in the City – I have to take some blame for that – to start, in his words, "making my fortune".

It had been all very amicable between us, but he left home as soon as he had sufficient funds to maintain a smart rented flat and Angela and I saw precious little of him over the following ten years. He would turn up now and again, usually unexpectedly and always with a different glamorous girl on his arm. I would never forget bumping into an acquaintance of Tom's at a seminar and him showing me several pages in a glossy porn magazine. I recognised the naked woman straight away; she had shared a family Sunday lunch at home with us not a month previously. At the time I did not know whether to be outraged or jealous.

This was the son that I had agreed to harbour in my cottage in rural Herefordshire; a convicted fraudster and proven philanderer. But, above all that, he was my son and I loved him.

The ensuing two weeks dragged by with me in a state of mixed excitement and trepidation. I told Sam that Tom was on his way but stopped short of revealing details of his misdemeanours. If that information were to be slipped into the conversation between the old codgers in the Tap Room it would be through the village and far away in no time at all. In other words, the cat would be out of the bag.

I might have guessed that Tom would just turn up on my doorstep. That was his way. I was so pleased to see him that I didn't think to chide his thoughtlessness. I hugged him unashamedly.

What a good looking man he was; blonde hair, blue eyes, six foot plus, and a body that reflected that he had joined the fitness fanatics in the Open Prison. Adversity had not robbed him of his easy smile and the few wrinkles on his tanned face could only be described as laughter lines. 'Good humour and fun' was his facial promise.

The second bedroom I had assigned to him was unusually large for a Victorian country cottage and that quickly became Tom's domain and he came to disappear there for most of the day. Just days after his appearance he had a second, dedicated telephone line installed and he borrowed my car to nip off to Birmingham to buy all manner of electronic equipment. He forged an agreement with me that his bedroom would be his space and that I would only enter by invitation. What could I do otherwise?

His only ongoing concession was to come down to the kitchen and share an early evening meal with me. That included the days that Sam would turn up and the two of them hit it off straight away. I had rarely seen the old man smile, let alone chuckle, but Tom held the magic key and positively enjoyed unlocking Sam's suppressed emotions. And Denzil too, now able to jump up onto laps, was torn between Tom and me – never Sam.

Tom liked our cider and could match Sam's appetite for the liquor "harn" by "harn". Whilst Sam would start wheezing and clicking his tongue after a quart or more, Tom showed no ill effects and unscrupulously encouraged the old shepherd unless I was quick enough to intervene. Inevitably, one day Sam threw his despicable cap on the floor and asked Tom if he thought "that yon kitty" could pick it up. I glanced across at Denzil and he knew exactly what to expect – I could see it in his eyes and the way he had shaped his tail – straight upright. I could also see that the cat, not wishing to be a party pooper, had resigned himself to the inevitable rather than flee. I came to his rescue and gave Sam the sharp end of my tongue.

Tom did not discuss with me the nature of his activities in what he termed his "office" but the explosion in the size of our postbag told me much. Using a telephonic share dealing service Tom was playing the stock market. I had dabbled a little myself so I knew the ropes on that one. It took me longer to cotton on to the fact that he was in contact with many of his old chums in the City, and beyond, and presumably receiving information to benefit the process of his buying and selling speculations.

Tentatively I did bring up the subject of Insider Dealing when we were alone in the kitchen one evening. "It's a criminal offence," I reminded him. "You could go straight back to prison if you get caught and it won't be a Category D next time."

"Don't worry Dad," Tom smiled easily, "there's no chance of that. I am not getting information that is privileged in any way. It's just odds and sods that are in the public domain."

I did not believe him but what could I do? Or say? I tried a different tack instead. "How come you can afford all this? The courts bankrupted you as part of your sentence. I had expected you to tap me up for a loan at the very least?"

I could see Tom picking his words. "Let's just say that I had a few quid stashed abroad that happened to escape the attention of the Office of the Official Receiver."

"That's fraud in itself," I fumed.

"Oh fuck off Dad and get a life."

That was about as close as we ever came that year to an out and out argument. To avoid such I backed off. That's what Dads do isn't it?

Easter came and went and April daffodils were in abundance when my son started courting again. Not before he went out by taxi one day and came back with a nearly new Aston Martin. I had been surprised that, as a discharged bankrupt, Tom had managed to obtain a U.K. bank account and so was amazed at how he had managed to get enough finance to buy a flash car.

"Finance Dad? Give it a rest. I paid cash. What do you think that I've been earning these past few weeks? Peanuts?"

Cometh the car, cometh the girl. Not a succession of them this time – but Jazz made up for a whole troupe. She was a redhead in her late twenties at a guess, not at the ginger end of the colour scale but chestnut; long and luxuriant. I would learn that she had a pattern book of style in her genes. Her clothes either just about hid the necessaries or otherwise glued to then to accentuate the contours. Sexy or what? And she knew it – which made her all the more sexy. I had sort of given up all pretentions in that department but, my word, Jazz brought thoughts and feelings tumbling back again.

And that flipping kitten Denzil. Hardly a kitten now – much more a cat. Whenever Jazz showed her face in the kitchen Denzil abandoned everyone and everything else. He would go close to berserk, rolling over in the hope of a tummy tickling session or engaging in aggravated attempts to gain her lap and from there her caresses. And of course, Jazz gave the wee man much of the attention he craved.

The first night that Jazz stayed over I knew that there was going to be ongoing trouble. The internal walls of the cottage were substantial and well sound proofed and the bedroom doors made of thick pitch pine. Nevertheless neither, on both sides of the landing, could contain the exuberant noises that emanated Tom's bed and which too often carried on what seemed half the night. Jazz's screams of encouragement together with Tom's grunts and laughter, I swear, rattled my windows. I did not actually hear the word "Geronimo" but there were, I am sure, several unidentifiable modern day equivalents.

Me, jealous? Of course not. Well... perhaps a little. Mmmm... on reflection, perhaps more than that.

Three week-ends later I had had quite enough. Jazz was fast becoming a permanent fixture – at week-ends. She had a week-day job in a boutique somewhere in Central London and the routine had become her arriving on Friday evening and leaving before dawn on Mondays. She drove a zippy Golf GTI. That in itself was a bone of contention as, often or not, she boxed me in. To add insult to injury, Jazz had had her exhaust doctored to produce a mighty roar on take-off which inevitably shot me out of the deepest of sleeps every Monday morning. I had to have words with my son.

Thankfully, Tom beat me to the draw and saved my blushes. Unusually he appeared at the breakfast table one morning to join me for coffee. "I've been thinking Dad. It might be a good idea if Jazz and I gave you some space." That was a good way of putting it. "How about I buy a caravan and put it in a corner of the orchard? Jazz and I could use it to sleep in at week-ends?"

Needless to say I jumped at his suggestion.

Later we explored my territory in search of the best site for a caravan. There were any manner of negatives with the orchard. Getting a caravan sited would be difficult because of low branches and access on foot would be a challenge – especially in fancy high heels. We had to agree that top spot was the wild part of the garden, close to the cottage but far enough away noise wise. Also the caravan would not be visible from the lane should its siting be of interest to the Planning Authorities.

Not for Tom, a pick and spade and wheelbarrow to clear the land. He had a contractor's three lads doing the work the very next day. A caravan, second hand but expensive, arrived on a transporter the day after. An electrician ran an overhead wire from the cottage and a temporary water supply utilised my garden hose. The transformation was complete in time for Jazz's next appearance and come the week-end I believed that I was to enjoy sleepful nights.

It is a privilege to own an orchard, however small. The fact that mine contained only cider apple trees was a relic from the past when cider was so very much part of Herefordshire country life. After all, it was within living memory that cider often formed part of an agricultural worker's wages. Whilst the Cornish workers had their pasties, the Herefordshire boys were sent off with bread and cheese and a costrel of cider – that being a small wooden barrel with a handle like a rotund handbag.

Nevertheless I had determined to re-plant the empty spaces in my orchard with fruit trees of other descriptions; desert and culinary apples, pears, plums, an apricot and perhaps a cherry or two. But I had missed the boat. Most of the trees were already in virgin leaf and the others, "lates", were still at the stage of mouse ears – buds newly opened. Maybe next season? I kidded myself that I had also missed the opportunity of a winter pruning exercise but I had deliberately put that to the back of my mind. Again, perhaps next winter.

My next problem would be keeping the orchard grass under control. There was no way I was going to struggle with the hand mower I had inherited from the previous owner to cut the manageable lawn in the cottage's garden. A ride-on mower or sheep? – that was the question. That was something that I needed to discuss with Sam.

I felt optimistic; dangerously self-satisfied even. I had had a lucky life – apart from losing Angela that is. If she were here, life would be perfect. My son was back together again in every respect and my daughter happily married in Australia. And I was a man with an orchard... Oh, in that moment of self-congratulation I completely forgot my late friend Peter.

Jazz had taken a half day off work that next Friday and arrived at Well Cottage in time to inspect the caravan and then be in the kitchen to greet Sam on his scheduled arrival. "I love the caravan," she blurted enthusiastically, "and I'm going to call it the *Nooky Kabin.*" Tom guffawed, I smiled and Sam looked totally bewildered.

"You know when a tup finds an ewe in season..." I offered a sheep analogy. I had never seen Sam blush, and I am not entirely sure that he did at that moment, but I think that he was put out by his need of an explanation when the rest of us knew exactly what nooky meant.

"It's enough to make a donkey break his bridle," Sam said lamely.

The caravan was not so christened that night. I was to endure yet another tempestuous night. The caravan needed "properly commissioning" to use Tom's expression. That meant bed linen and crockery and goodness know what else and all purchased the following day. For me that meant peace, glorious peace was just in the offing.

And so a new routine became established. Tom took to sleeping in the caravan full time but used his erstwhile bedroom as an office during the day – and often long into evenings when Jazz was not around. Even from the kitchen downstairs I could hear his telephone ringing pretty well constantly which made me wonder whether playing the stock market should engender that level of external communication. Tom kept a tight lip when it came to his business activities and I continued to take a line of least resistance and left him to it.

Mid May and the blossom in the orchard was an absolute picture. I had learned from the village shop that there was an apiarist in a neighbouring village and his bees had only a short distance to travel in order to plunder the nectar and help assist in ensuring a good Autumn harvest. Sam put a downer on that idea in his inimitable way. "If there be a field of rape anywhere near they'll be off after it. 'Tis easier pickings." Happily, Sam's foreboding of a late frost did not materialise. "Jack Frost can kill an 'arvest stone dead."

I did not particularly enjoy the double varietal cider, Yarlington Mills' with Ten Commandments, and I suspect that Sam was of the same mind – but would not admit to being so. Tom and Jazz were not of the same opinion as me and I was pleased to see a plastic keg, and later another, disappear through the door of the *Nooky Kabin*. Of the main body of the cider there was one barrel still untapped and a second which Sam decanted into plastic kegs as soon as they became available. "Don't do too much good air getting to it?" Sam explained. I reckoned that bringing a plastic keg up the cellar stairs once a week cut short his need to descend down there.

"The drop's a good un." announced Sam one Saturday in June after a stormy night before.

"The drop?"

"Aye, come and see." I followed the old man out into the orchard. "See, all them bits on the ground." I wandered through the tree and under many of them were scattered amongst the grass little apples the size of large peas, with their associated stalks – sort of like miscarriages.

"What's wrong? Have they got a disease or something?" To me it seemed a major loss of harvest. Sam deliberately left me in the dark and watched me wander under the trees with an ever sinking heart. Either he became bored of the spectacle or he took pity on me.

"Naw, 'tis a good sign. It means there's too much for the trees to take. Them on the floor's the offloads. – what are too many for the tree."

"Well Sam, one learns something new every day."

Soon after that I came down one Sunday morning to find Tom and Jazz sitting at the kitchen table. This was so rare an occurrence as to be unheard of. I rarely saw either of them before noon on a Sunday. I had the feeling that they were sat there waiting for me and with something of importance to tell me. I was correct in that assumption.

"You're not going to believe this Dad," started Tom excitedly. I sat down eyeing the kettle and the tea caddy from that distance. "You know when I had that corner of the garden cleared for the caravan? Well, one of the lads brought me an old telephone that he had found in the undergrowth." I groaned and my facial expression became pained. Tom picked up on that immediately and asked, "You knew that it was there?"

"Yes," I said simply. "I did. I'd forgotten about it."

"A French phone, old, vintage?" added Jazz.

I nodded. "I brought it back from France last year." I just hoped that I was wrong about what I expected was to come next.

"Jazz fell in love with it, polished it up and it has stood pride of place in an alcove since we moved into the caravan. I didn't realise that it belonged to you."

"That's O.K.," I said. "Is that all?"

"Well, no. It's the darndest thing, Dad. It rang – last night."

"What time?" I asked.

That was obviously not the reply that either Tom or Jazz had expected. Puzzled my son said, "Why do you ask that?"

"Just tell me what time, son?"

Tom and Jazz consulted each other and agreed "Just after eleven."

"That's different. Did you lift the receiver and listen?"

"Tom was scared to but I did," answered Jazz proudly.

"No way was I scared," protested Tom unconvincingly. "You were just nearer than I was."

"On your life," Jazz taunted.

"O.K., never mind all that," I intervened. "Was there anybody on the end of the line?"

"Yes there was," said the girl. "How can that be? There's no wires connecting it to anything unless it has been converted to a mobile somehow. We couldn't find any electronics for that and we virtually took the thing to bits afterwards."

"Afterwards?"

"A woman kept going on about being drowned with her baby. She kept asking for help. Tom, who was listening on the separate earpiece by then, grabbed the receiver off me and she said the same to him."

Tom nodded. "I asked her where she was and she said something about a pond in the cottage here. I could not make sense of it and then the voice suddenly cut off and that was that."

The pond here? I vaguely remembered Sam mentioning a pond and a drowning the first time that I had set eyes on him. Time to think. I stood up and made myself a coffee, offering Tom and Jazz some too. What should I do next? They were both intelligent adults after all and probably had a right to know. I fed Denzil who was meowing for his breakfast, although torn between his stomach and showering his affection on Jazz. I handed out the coffee I had made; three cups. Only then did I sit back down at the table and, uttering a long sigh of resignation, "I have an unusual and harrowing story to tell you both."

CHAPTER EIGHT

I related the story of my visiting France and buying the telephone at a vide grenier, my erstwhile friend Peter, the Mustang pilot, contacting the American War Museum, the WZRG and finally the bomb and its disastrous consequences. I tacked on my and Tom's mother's experience with the Ouija board séance and my suspicions about evil spirits at work. Tom and Jazz listened with hardly an interruption. By the time I had finished, my coffee had turned cold and Denzil was trying his hardest to gain Jazz's lap. For once she appeared oblivious to his endeavours.

"Bloody hell," was the best that Tom could come up with.

"I should have thrown that phone in the River Wye or something even more permanent. Goodness knows what possessed me to just lob it into a corner of the garden," I breathed apologetically.

Later that day Jazz tracked me down. "Tom and I have had a long chat about what we should do with the French telephone. We're going to see what happens next Saturday; see, if as you say, it rings at the same time. If it does, or it doesn't, we will decide where to go from there."

I knew then that I should have over-ridden her; told her that the telephone belonged to me and that I wanted to regain possession. But I was not dealing with two children but a couple of free thinking adults and I did not want to give cause for a serious confrontation. I did not think that a delay of one week would do too much harm. I have to admit that I was distracted by a problem closer to my heart. I had Sam to thank for that.

"That there cat wants cutting."

It really hadn't occurred to me that Denzil should be neutered. From a male perspective there was nowt so precious as one's genitals. "Once he gits a taste for shaggin' he'll be off. See if 'e don't. And e'll spray and all." I made an appointment with the same veterinary surgery in Leominster to which I had taken Denzil to for his routine injections.

Despite Sam's assurances to the contrary I was worried that post-operation Denzil would experience a long period of recovery and, worse still, he would resent me for depriving him of his manhood. I need not have worried on either score as his ten minutes under the vet's scalpel had few adverse effects and I still remained very much his chum.

Back at the turn of the year an ex-City pal of mine, a fellow widower, had invited me for a week's holiday in Spain. The catch was that he needed a co-driver to help take his caravan to a holiday camp site near Alicante. I was to spend a week on site with him and then catch a plane back to the U.K. alone. I had agreed all too easily and not given the matter too much further thought. A telephone call from Jim reminding me that passage to Spain was booked for that coming Sunday was quite a shock. How could I let him down, especially as he had taken on himself to book, and pay for, my flight home?

Tom agreed to look after Denzil, and for that matter Sam too, with alacrity. That Sunday afternoon saw me in the familiar surroundings of Portsmouth Ferry Terminal but on this occasion waiting to board the Brittany Ferries sailing to Santander. The Jim that I knew of old had had a penchant for alcohol in any one of its many guises and nothing had changed. From teatime to bedtime I was obliged to keep him company in the ship's comfortable bar and, whilst I was fairly abstemious, Jim happily took up the remains of my notional share. Sharing a windowless cabin with a grossly inebriated man intent on snoring his way through the night was no sinecure and more than a dozen times I chided myself for being caught in such a situation.

Happily the Bay of Biscay did not live up to its stormy reputation and the voyage took just over the twenty-four hours that it was scheduled to be. Jim insisted on driving most of the journey to a hotel on the outskirts of Madrid despite the fact, I had warned he was likely to have failed a breathalyser test. He was known for his pigheadedness. I took the home straight to the holiday site near Alicante. I should have guessed that the rendezvous with fellow caravaners was effectively a pre-school holiday piss-up and a number of the participants were known to me, if only by their faces. There we had some good times, and I worked on tanning my body in the agreeable Spanish sun, but I was relieved to eventually board the Easyjet flight to Bristol Airport.

Sitting on the train from Temple Meads to Hereford my thoughts wandered to the French telephone and from there to concerns that nothing untoward had happened in my absence. I had been away from the cottage for two Saturdays and that probably meant that Tom and Jazz had two opportunities to field mischievous calls from the drowned woman if the routine followed that of the Mustang pilot. I had, of course, spoken to Tom on my mobile to warn him of my pending return but I had not thought to mention the French telephone. Or had I cowardly ducked the issue?

Late evening a taxi dropped me back to Well Cottage where, to my relief, I found Tom in the lounge happily watching television with Denzil curled up beside him. We exchanged pleasantries, enjoyed a nightcap together and I went off to bed, very glad to be in my own pit. Home sweet home.

I slept in the following morning and ten o'clock showed on my bedside clock as I made my way down stairs. I could hear Tom on the telephone in his week-day bedroom cum office – nothing unusual there. Denzil was cross at having had to wait for his breakfast – nothing unusual there either. What was unusual, when I sat down with coffee and toast, was the urgent banging on the front door. Who the hell could that be?

Two burly policemen in flat caps and yellow hazard jackets, Traffic Cops I guessed, appraised me professionally. I realised afterwards that they must have been weighing up as to whether I was the object of their intrusion. Having apparently decided that I was not, the lead policeman concluded that a reasonably polite approach was called for. "We would like a word with Mr. Thomas Rupert Harper. Is he on the premises, please, Sir?"

"Why yes," I stammered. "He's my son."

"Mind if we come inside, Sir?" It was hardly a request as the officer was already pushing forward causing me to step aside. I pointed towards the kitchen door and the three of us assembled there.

"What's this about?" I asked automatically

"We just need a chat with your son, please Sir," said the second officer softly.

Denzil tried to introduce himself to the policemen but was completely ignored.

"Tom's upstairs, I'll give him a shout." I stepped out into the hall and shouted up the stairs. One of the officers had half followed me. "Tom, Tom, there's a couple of policemen here who want to see you."

Tom heard me and came out of his room to look down over the banisters. He could hardly have failed to see the officer standing in the hall. For just a split second I thought that Tom was about to dive back into his bedroom and I had the impression that the policeman did too. "O.K. I'll be right down." Thankfully he descended the stairs and we all re-assembled in the kitchen.

"Are you Thomas Rupert Harper?" asked the first officer. Tom nodded. "I have an arrest warrant in your name, Mr. Harper. You must accompany us to the police station in Leominster. I am afraid, for security reasons, I must handcuff you."

"Fucking hell," I half shouted, "What's he supposed to have done to deserve this sort of treatment?"

Tom looked totally bemused.

"The warrant states threatening behaviour," said the second officer. "That's all we know. Our job is just to bring him into custody."

"What, in fucking handcuffs?"

"I believe that your son is out on licence from Springside Open Prison." explained Officer 1. "Tom appears to have contravened the conditions of his parole and we don't take any chances with convicted criminals," he added with relish.

Tom looked at me helplessly. This was not the son that I knew and loved. He looked defeated and there was not an ounce of resistance in him. The couple of years that he had spent as a guest of Her Majesty had obviously taken their toll in that department.

"If you contact the police station in Leominster later today you can probably arrange to see your son," said the more conciliatory Officer. With that they fair marched Tom out of the house and whisked him away.

The cottage was deathly quiet until Tom's telephone started ringing in his office upstairs. If that was one of his investment chums then perhaps there was a financial transaction in the offing that was doomed to fail.

I deliberately allowed several hours to pass. I reasoned that Tom would be processed through the police's system and then questioned. My son was sensible enough to insist on having a lawyer present if that should prove necessary. A legal expert would do more for him that I could. By two o'clock I was sufficiently fraught to jump into my car and take off for Leominster.

The Custody Sergeant was placatory. "On the scale of things the complaint against your son is not that heinous. Because he is on licence from the Open Prison technically he should be returned to Sussex until this matter is sorted out one way or another. Inspector Roberts has taken a pragmatic view and is allowing your son to be under a loose house arrest pending the outcome of our investigations. If you care to take a seat Mr. Harper, I'll see if I can speed up his release."

After two hours spent positioning my bum on an unyielding plastic chair and two cups of grotty machine engineered coffee, Tom appeared, free to leave. I drove him home with hardly a word passing between us, quite deliberately so. The kitchen table in Well Cottage was to be the venue for the forthcoming inquisition.

"The Saturday night after you had left for Spain the French phone rang much as you said it would – shortly after eleven o'clock. The same voice, a woman, same story, of being drowned with her baby. This time she made it clear that she had been pregnant – the baby hadn't been born. She said that her lover had done it. Her lover had deliberately drowned her.

Jazz was really upset by this. You may have an idea as to what she's like – gets a real bee in her bonnet – especially over women's matters. She said that we had to do something about it. We just could not ignore that the woman had been murdered. I said that we didn't know for sure but she quoted you, Dad. Your story of the Mustang pilot was proved true wasn't it?"

"Sort of," I had to agree.

"When you were in Spain, Jazz took the week off work and I was expected to as well. The voice had said to us, the first time we heard it, that there had been a pond in the cottage's grounds. I remember that you didn't disagree?"

I nodded. I had meant to brooch the subject with Sam and it had slipped my mind.

"Jazz visited the Herefordshire Records Office and found maps confirming that there had been a natural pond in the garden here. At the Hereford Times Office she pulled out newsprint reporting the drowning of Christine Palmer in 1987 – not that long ago. The coroner's verdict was suicide, no doubt influenced by her being pregnant and unmarried. The Palmer parents sold up and moved close to Taunton – that address we obtained from the Land Registry at Telford. Jazz contacted them and they gave us, after some cajoling, the information we needed.

We drove down to Somerset and found the Palmers in a cottage very similar to yours, Dad. We told them a cock and bull story about how there was a doubt that their daughter had committed suicide – we could hardly tell them about the French telephone. Mr. Palmer couldn't take any more and would have nothing more to do with us. But his wife was attracted to vengeance – not half she was. Anyway she said that Christine had a boyfriend called Terence, Terry Hall and he was a real randy little sod. Christine confided to her sister that Terry was constantly trying to get her knickers off. Mrs. Palmer said of Christine that her daughter was determined to walk into church on her wedding day a virgin. The conclusion was that Terry had his way in the end; that Christine found herself pregnant and could not live with the fact.

Jazz asked if she knew how we could find this Terence Hall. Mrs Palmer still had contact with friends in this area and had heard that he had married and lived in Kington on the Welsh border. Jazz spent the next day trying to track him down. It wasn't difficult. He's married with four children and living in near poverty by the looks of his house.

I went to see him. I insisted that I went alone. For a start I couldn't trust Jazz to keep her temper and I didn't want to place her in danger anyway. I didn't know what the bloke might be capable of – especially if he had drowned Christine Palmer. I found him in a rundown council house with junk everywhere – inside and outside. He was very suspicious of me from the start – not that I could blame him for that."

"Who did you say you were? Did you pass yourself off as a policeman or something like?"

Tom looked distinctly embarrassed. "No, I didn't go that far. I said that I was a private investigator – which I suppose I was. I was investigating and am a private person."

"Bit farfetched," I murmured. "Anyway, go on."

"Terry admitted that he had been trying to bed Christine virtually from the first time that they went out together. He also admitted to having a very strong sex drive. Those are my words – his were a damned sight more graphic. According to him Christine would have none of it and was determined to hang onto her virginity. Or was until just before she died. His story is that she came on to him in a big way, begging him – er – have intercourse with her. Terry put that more crudely as you might imagine."

"And did he?"

"Not according to him. He was already seeing another girl and was about to tell Christine to shove off, or something similar. He has a very vulgar tongue. But he did say that when it came to light that Christine was three months pregnant when she died, he was deeply shocked. She had been messing about with another man – of that he was in no doubt.

"The inference is completely out of character, Christine had wanted Terry to have sex with her just before she drowned in order to pass off the baby as his. Desperate measures."

"And that's it?"

"Yes Dad, I swear. I won't say that the meeting was convivial in the least. I thanked him and left."

"So how come the complaint to the police?"

"Search me, Dad. I noticed his wife or partner taking down my car's number plate so that may be how I was traced. Given time to think, Terry Hall must have taken offence at my visit. What other reason can there be? I think it likely that he was telling me the truth."

"Your turning up there driving an Aston Martin probably did little to help your cause."

"I didn't think of that at the time," agreed Tom.

My instinct was to go down the garden to the caravan, retrieve the French telephone, smash it to smithereens, collect the bits and straight away dispose of then in the Council Tip. I put that idea to my son. He appeared to contemplate my suggestion for quite some time, weighing up the pros and cons.

"It's Friday, Dad, and Jazz will be here come the evening. Before we do anything rash I think that we'd be wise to involve her. She ought to have a say in the matter because she's really emotionally involved. I don't know how she would react if we destroyed the telephone."

I wanted to say that Jazz was not a permanent fixture at Well Cottage and that I was and it was my prerogative, and mine alone, to take whatever action which I thought best. And to a lesser extent that applied to Tom too. But I backed off that possible field of conflict convincing myself that delaying the execution by a day or two could do little harm.

Sam turned up at teatime and I pounced on him to tell me about the pond that had once been a feature in my garden. "Been there as long as I can remember. Fed by an underground spring I reckon. Deep it were. Took a lot of filling in after the Palmer girl died." He knew little else of importance to me and I hurried him through a couple of glasses of cider as politely as I could.

I heard Jazz arrive – I could hardly fail to with the modification of her exhaust – and glimpsed her walking past the kitchen door on her way down the garden to the caravan. Half an hour later she and Tom settled themselves either end of the kitchen table. Tom had obviously primed her as to what was afoot.

"You can't destroy the telephone instrument Desmond," she waded in straight away. "We need to ask Christine more questions – especially after what this Terry Hall has told Tom."

"You had the chance to do that last Saturday night didn't you?" I retorted.

"No, we didn't. Last week-end we spent the time together in London. Didn't he tell you?"

"So you have had only the two contacts with this Christine woman?"

"Yes."

"And you don't even know whether she tried to contact you at elevenish last Saturday night?"

"All the more reason for us to see whether she does tomorrow, Desmond."

I found that logic difficult to deny. Eventually I agreed to delay a decision until that Sunday morning on the condition that I was present in the caravan late on Saturday night.

I blamed myself for the situation we were in. I had had many opportunities to either destroy the telephone or, at least, divest myself of it. Instead I had dilly-dallied. My working life

I had been successful and I had put that down, in part, to my positivity. Where had that disappeared to? Was it a consequence of retirement? Or was it an age thing? Please don't let it be the consequence of Alzheimer's.

Duly, we three sat in silence the next night tensely watching the clock slide past the eleventh hour. Right on time the telephone rang in the French style. Ring… Ring… Jazz picked up the main handset before the third ring and I the earpiece extension. That was what we had planned to do.

"Help me, help me." The cry was all too familiar; a carbon copy of pilot Ricci, apart from it being a female voice.

"Who are you?" asked Jazz.

"Christine, Christine Palmer."

"Where are you??"

"He drowned me and my baby, help me, help me."

"Who drowned you?" That was the key question ,.

"My lover, drowned me in the pond."

"What's your lover's name?" Jazz demanded to know, tension obvious in her voice.

"Help me, help me. He drowned me and my baby."

Three more times Jazz asked the question and three more times she received the same non-reply. My instincts told me that, from my experience with Ricci, the time limit was shortly to expire. I roughly grabbed the handset from Jazz's hand and shouted into it, "Who the fucking hell is your lover?"

There was a longish silence. I thought that the line had disconnected much as I had expected it to do. Then a plaintive voice said quietly, "I love pasta." There was nothing after that.

Jazz could hardly not have noticed the frowns on my countenance. She had not had the wit to pick up the earpiece and hear Christine's final words. "I love pasta."

"I love pasta." Did I hear right? What had that to do with a drowned woman.

All three of us grabbed at the suggestion of a stiff drink and, rather than repair up to the cottage, we settled on Jazz's tipple of gin and slimline tonic. Luckily she had brought a full litre bottle back from London. That took us the best part of two hours to see off; two hours of quite fierce negotiations.

My position was crystal clear. I wanted to sweep the whole thing under the carpet, destroy the telephone set, dispense with the pieces and try and forget that it had ever happened. My problem would be in living with the certain knowledge that a young, pregnant woman had drowned herself only a matter of yards from my bedroom window. If I could not put that behind me, given time, ultimately I would have to sell Well Cottage and move on.

Jazz on the other hand, becoming more persistent as the level in the gin bottle declined, was all for reaching out to third parties for support and guidance. At various stages of our conversation she suggested involving the police, Social Services, a clairvoyant and an exorcist…then back to the police again. I argued that nobody would believe such an improbable story to which Jazz replied that any doubters only had to listen in on one Saturday night to be convinced. And Jazz was adamant that she had the powers of persuasion to get the authorities to do just that.

Her convictions brought forth an even worse scenario as far as I was concerned. If it were to be established by competent authorities as a true phenomenon, the world-wide press could have an absolute heyday. I could become famous and infamous; the icon of a religious sect on one part and a harbinger of the Devil on another. My life would never be my own again. And that could possibly become the lot of Jazz and Tom as well. These wild predictions, of course, were fuelled by gin.

The possibility of celebrity status, whatever the route that led there, excited Jazz greatly; her dream come true. Thankfully Tom started to get my point and came to my aid if only because he was concerned about the future of his relationship with Jazz. This argument reeled Jazz in a measure and when I shared the last of the gin between our three glasses we had a consensus that I would attempt to go and talk to Mrs. Palmer in Somerset to see if I could shed further light on Christine's mysterious lover.

During their visit to the Palmer household, Mrs. Palmer had volunteered her telephone number to Jazz making it clear that she expected to be updated. Jazz was sure that she would be amenable to a visit from me.

I hit the sack that night with many misgivings but nevertheless with some relief. I would telephone Mrs. Palmer in the morning and if she proved agreeable, make my way down to Somerset post haste.

CHAPTER NINE

Burton Harvey must have been an attractive village in its day. A medieval church stood testament to the age of the stone built dwellings that clustered around and about a central cross-roads. At that point a public house, the Hopton Arms, had positioned itself to take on the twenty-first century with a gaudy offer of "two meals for the price of one" including a free drink. Unfortunately for Burton Harvey this piece of Olde England was now surrounded by new housing estates; dormitories for nearby Taunton no doubt.

"Fair View", home to the Palmers was, as Tom had said, similar in shape to Well Cottage but close to the transition between the old village and the dull red bricks of one of the older housing estates. Mrs. Palmer answered the door with such expedition to suggest that she had been peeking out of her lounge window in anticipation of my arrival.

"Call me Elizabeth," she replied to my introduction. "Liz if you like."

That was friendly enough and very encouraging. I asked after her husband but, as I had come to expect, he had made himself scarce. I took no real notice of the excuses that Liz made for him.

"Christine was a quiet girl, timid – took after her father in that respect. We had lots of trouble with her being bullied at school. That stopped in the fifth form when she found a champion in Terry Hall. He appointed himself as her protector.

Goodness knows he was as rough as they come and fearless when it came to fighting. Chris was really grateful as you can imagine and after they both left school she sort of adopted him as her boyfriend."

"Sort of, how do you mean?" I interrupted.

"Terry was seeing other girls and sowing wild oats. At one time he was having an affair with a married woman nearly twice his age in Hereford, so I was told. He was a modern day Don Juan in a coarse sort of way. Christine knew this but it didn't seem to bother her. But I do know that she didn't join his chorus of conquests – well – not until the last six months of her life that is."

"How can you be sure about that Liz?"

"We had a very close relationship and could talk to each other about just about anything. And we did. Can I trust you with a huge secret?"

"Absolutely."

"I had a short fling with the then landlord of the Dog and Duck. On Ladies Darts Nights, I was flinging off more than my arrows. Christine new all about it and we often had a little snigger together. Believe me, Desmond, if Christine had been intimate with Terry Hall I would have known. "

"I see," I said, taken aback by the woman's candidness.

"That's until six months before she died. She changed. I knew my daughter and she was holding something back from me. That must have been when she surrendered to Terry Hall and the bastard got her pregnant. "

"My son went to see Terry at his home in Kington. You kindly found the address for him."

"That's right, I did."

"Terry admits trying to get his end away with Christine for years. He makes absolutely no bones about that. Christine's answer, according to him, was that she wanted to approach the altar on her wedding day as a virgin. Yet shortly before she committed suicide, according to Terry's version of things, Christine threw herself at him virtually begging for him to make love to her."

"Well, that explains how she became pregnant," said Liz austerely.

"No, the autopsy said she was three months pregnant or thereabouts. According to Terry Christine only started to come onto him about two weeks before she died."

"He's obviously lying," said the mother, her anger flaring.

"Could there have been other boys or men that she might have had a fling with?"

"Absolutely not. Apart from with Terry she never went out anywhere. He would always collect her in his fancy car and bring her home again. She had no opportunity to meet other men."

"Never went anywhere?"

"Well, she went shopping in the daytime to Hereford and Leominster and often I would go with her. She had a part-time job in the village shop which gave her spending money. The only other place that she went regularly was to church. She was a devout Christian. I don't know where she got that from – not from her father or me."

"She attended St. Edmund's in the village?"

"What, with that pervert of a bloody Rector? Thank God he's gone to his grave. No, she attended a church in Harcross. Every Sunday without fail and a couple of evenings for bible reading if she could get her Dad to loan her the car."

"My son and his girlfriend told you that there was some doubt in their minds that Christine had committed suicide?"

"Yes, the girl, Jasmine, said that she had been to a séance and come away with that idea."

"She told you what she heard."

"Yes, it wasn't much." The woman repeated the story that Jazz and Tom had told me, the ones they had heard on the telephone that first Saturday.

"No," I agreed, "it isn't much at all. I think that it must be a red herring."

"You don't think that your son and girlfriend are just out to cause mischief?" asked the woman with suspicion written on her face.

"Absolutely not Liz. For a start I know my son very well."

"And I thought that I knew Christine well too," Liz interrupted, "but I apparently didn't."

"Tom went to challenge Terry Harper who afterwards made a complaint to the police with the result that Tom was arrested and may be facing charges."

"Hmmm." said Liz, unconvinced.

"If this is a wild goose chase then I am really, really sorry."

Just as I taking my leave a thought struck me. "Did Christine love eating pasta?"

"Pasta?

"Spaghetti and the like?"

Elizabeth took time to think. "Not particularly. We would eat it in some form or another now and again. I wouldn't have said it was a favourite food of hers."

"Oh well, just a thought."

"That's a funny question to ask. What are you getting at?"

I could hardly mention the incident the previous night on the French telephone, having put down the contact with Christine to have occurred during a séance. Jazz had mentioned something about Christine loving pasta. I probably got that wrong." I determined that it would be best if I changed the direction of the conversation. "Where were you and your husband on the day that Christine died?"

"We were on holiday that week with our other daughter Jennifer, Christine's younger sister. We were to have a week in the Mumbles but of course we had to cut that short."

"Christine didn't want to go with you?"

"No. That was the first time that she hadn't come on holiday with us. She said that she wanted some time on her own and we went along with it."

"Was the pond very deep – it can't have been that big?"

"No, at most the water would have come up as far as Chris's waist. But, as the police pointed out to me, people can drown in six inches of water – especially if they have a mind to."

"Did Christine confide in you that she was pregnant, Elizabeth?"

"No." Tears welled up in the woman's eyes for the first time. "The first we knew was from the results of the autopsy. If only we had known…" I reached into my pocket to try and find a tissue but Liz pulled herself together. "We'd have stood by her, I know we would."

"Was Christine buried or cremated?"

That question caused the woman more distress. She could hardly answer, "We buried her in Hereford. My heart breaks that we cannot visit her regularly. It's such a distance from here."

I left Elizabeth Palmer with distress written large across her eyes. My heart went out to her; it could hardly do otherwise in the circumstances.

I arrived back at Well Cottage in the early evening and was soon joined in my kitchen by Tom and Jasmine. "You've just missed Sam," said Tom by way of greeting, "and we've fed Denzil."

I related the events of my time in Somerset as comprehensively as I could. We chewed the information through and through until there was no taste left in the gum, as it were. If Terry Hall had drowned Christine Palmer there was not a shred of evidence that would stand up in a court of law. There was no clue whatsoever there was anyone else involved.

By far the most pressing concern for me was the complaint that Hall had made to the police that could lead to Tom being yanked back to prison in default of his parole.

My best advice was to forget about Christine Palmer and destroy the French telephone. Then we should try and discover if Hall had engaged a solicitor to assist him in the matter of the complaint and if so Tom should attempt to deliver an abject apology through that solicitor in the hope that Terry Hall would withdraw his complaint. After all it was not the sort of offence that would likely result in Terry Hall receiving any financial compensation.

Jasmine was not to be easily persuaded and became agitated in her protestations. "We can't just run away from this. There must be something more that we can do surely?"

"Like what? " I challenged her with some irritation in my voice.

"We could ask to see the autopsy report and a transcript of the Coroner's Court Hearing. The autopsy showed that Christine was pregnant. Didn't anybody ask who the father of the baby was?"

"The parents assumed that it was Terry Hall."

"Yes, but weren't efforts made to confirm that? And did Hall know that he was in the frame? Surely he would have kicked up about that if he really hadn't been intimate with Christine, as he maintains now. After all, he's made a song and dance about Tom visiting him."

I was at a bit of a loss and my reply did not come quickly. "Terry was little more than a boy then. He's a good deal older now and even more street-wise. And I think that he was pushed into making a complaint by his wife or girlfriend or whatever. But anyway, so what if he were the father? That doesn't prove that he killed Christine."

"It would prove that he's a liar," protested Jazz. "And if he wasn't the father for sure then who the bloody hell is?"

"You're going off on a wild goose chase again, Jasmine, I know you are. DNA testing was in its infancy back then. They certainly would not have gone to those lengths as a matter of routine. The opportunity to prove the fatherhood has long gone."

"Come on Jazz, darling, you're going to have to let this go," said Tom soothingly.

"Was Christine buried or cremated?" Jazz blurted. I looked at her blankly. "Because if she was buried there might be a chance of DNA from what's left of the foetus."

"Highly unlikely," I replied wearily unwilling to disclose that I knew that she was buried in Hereford's main cemetery.

"There's a chance," urged the young woman.

"Can you imagine what red tape you would have to overcome to obtain permission for an exhumation? Be realistic Jazz – it's not going to happen."

The look of defiance on Jazz's face would have been appealing in different circumstances. My word, she was a fighter; her red hair and blazing green eyes were further testament to that. Tom had better keep his wits about him if he was lucky enough to be her long term boyfriend.

"A compromise," Tom chipped in. "Let's have one more go with the telephone next Saturday night."Let's ask Christine, or whoever it really is, the identity of the baby's father. If we get no further Jazz agrees to closure. If we get something positive we take it from there. How about that?"

I saw that as a practical if not a sensible way forward. I looked into Jazz's eyes as she did mine and there was tacit agreement of sorts. Yet Jazz had capitulated too easily for my peace of mind.

Denzil chose that exact moment to struggle through the cat flap with a dead-looking mouse in his mouth. This was the first of his kills that I was aware of and he was obviously extremely proud of himself. He looked up at me and then Jazz and chose to deliver his prize to the girl. After all she was his favourite. He laid the rodent at her feet whereupon it sat up, shook its head, and darted away. "Eek," squealed the girl, more in surprise than fear I guess, and for the next five minutes the three humans completely forgot about Christine and all connected with her.

The mouse? After a chase round the kitchen, it squeezed under the cellar door and by the time that I could click the latch to give a furious Denzil access the rodent had plenty of time to scoot. Not that it was needed, my brave cat was just as loathe to descend into the cellar as Sam was. That was the reason how Mr. (or Mrs.) Mouse lived on to see the light of another day.

At least that small episode served to clear our minds of Christine Palmer and we all went about the business of the day.

I could hardly fail to hear Jazz jump into her Golf GTI early the next morning to start a new week at the London boutique. Tom had obviously risen with her and I heard him come through the back door and up the stairs to his office. To all intent and purposes life was back to normal – except for that very black cloud hanging over my son's head.

I decided that I could do little harm to Tom's cause by visiting the police station in Leominster and try and find out what they might have in store for my son. The suspense was metaphorically killing us both and I reasoned that they may be more likely to speak to me than to him. If not then the best way forward might be to hire the services of a good lawyer. However, the sun was shining outside in a cloudless sky and, as I had had an arduous time in Somerset the day before I decided to mow the garden and orchard on the sit-on mower that I had recently acquired from a garden centre near Ross-on-Wye.

Sam heard the mower as he was passing by en route for a lunchtime harn or two in the Tap Room of the Dog and Duck, and he used that as an excuse to pop lean over the orchard gate. He was taken aback as to how pleased I was to see him especially so when I offered, cider, bread and cheese. "I want you to tell me all you know about Christine Palmer."

Sam scratched his head by slipping his hands under his filthy cap. "Nowt really, she kept 'erself to 'erself. Quiet little thing. I only knew 'er 'cos she took turns in the village shop."

"Did she have any friends that you know of?"

"None as I can remember – apart from that boy from 'ereford. 'E was a randy little fokker and no mistake."

"Do you remember his name?"

Sam lapsed into thought – or pretended to. "Naw gaffer," he said at last.

"I've heard the local gossip was that the boy was the father of Christine's baby?"

"Dunno," replied Sam noncommittally. "Can't say as I remember. Twas her sister what 'ad the reputation."

"Jennifer?"

"Yeh, Juicy Jenny. That's what the village lads called her. Leaves a lot to the imagination. Mind you, in me day, I'd 'ave given it some."

"Tell me about the pond, Sam. It wasn't that deep?"

"Naw. Bout meet my waist give or take. Took the girl some doing to drown 'erself."

"And Mr. Palmer had it filled in afterwards?"

"Yep. Where your lawn is now. No trace. I see'd the truck bringing the spoil the day it got filled in."

"How's the cider doing down the cellar?" I asked, completely changing the subject.

"The good stuff's going down. Plenty of the mixture left though."

"What you call the mixture was supposed to be a happy marriage between Yarlington Mills' and Ten Commandments. You said that they make a good drop of cider. I remember that well."

"Well…" Sam searched for an adequate excuse. "Mebbe it was a bad year. Can't always tell 'ow it'll turn out."

In the event I wrote on my shopping list the need to buy a couple of plastic casks of draught cider. They would be in place when we ran out of the good stuff.

Mid-afternoon Tom came flying down the stairs and found me wiping down the sit-on lawnmower after its successful toil."Jazz has just phoned me. She has had a conversation with the Coroner's Office in Gloucester. Evidently they cover the Herefordshire area. According to their records Christine's body was released for burial."

"We knew that already."

"But they're going to look into their records to see what blood samples were taken at the time."

I groaned. "That girl just doesn't give up does she?" Tom gave me a proud boyfriend smile. "We had agreed a way forward and that did not include contacting the coroner's office."

"She's set on getting justice for Christine."

"I know, and that's laudable but not if she opens a can of worms in the process."

"That's not a very good analogy Dad when talking about exhumation."

"I would have called it quite apt. Still, I'll not argue the point. I just hope that Jazz stops right there." Mulling over her latest initiative I was surprised that Jazz had not approached the police in an effort to support her beleaguered boyfriend. I would need to beat her to the gun.

Wednesday dawned promising another beautiful day and, on the spur of the moment, I decided to take a circuitous route to Leominster, one that would take me through the small settlement of Harcross. That was where Elizabeth Palmer had said Christine worshipped and I felt a strange urge to see for myself; something similar to walking in her footsteps I suppose.

Harcross was situated in a depression and the traveller approaching from any of the four roads leading thereto would have a hilltop view of the village and could hardly fail to notice, and be impressed by, the commanding spire of the church in the centre of a hodgepodge of houses. A posh sign erected next to the lytch gate importantly announced "Church of St. Ethelbert" and drew attention to its Norman connections. I parked the car and walked back, through the lytch gate and up the short path lined with monuments ascribed to the parish's once wealthiest residents – all dust for over a century or so.

Alas the imposing oak doors, studded with iron bolts, possibly Norman in age, refused to yield and I was obliged to settle for an external tour along a flagged pavement. I was halfway round when I crossed the path of a man, older than me I reckoned, who was clipping a small privet hedge. It would have been very rude of me not to have acknowledged him as I passed by, but there was no fear of that anyway. The man was eager to lay his clippers aside and engage me in conversation.

He started a diatribe about the history of his church and of St. Ethelbert the saint but was quick to appreciate my polite disinterest. Politics and sport were embraced for a while but the inevitability in the circumstances that I would bring Christine Palmer into the conversation duly won through.

"I'm born and bred in Harcross and lived here all my life. And this church has been my rock ever since I was a choir boy. I've never met or heard of a Christine Palmer. The congregation on a Sunday ain't that big, them's old and all regulars apart from a few holidaymakers in the summer. Your Christine would have stood out like a sore thumb."

"Her mother told me that Christine attended bible classes some evenings?"

"Ho, ho," my companion laughed heartily. "That certainly wasn't at St. Ethelbert's Sunday School nor nowhere else. I tell you, you're barking up a wrong tree mister."

CHAPTER TEN

I did not receive a joyous reception at Leominster police station; a blank wall would have been a better description although the pimply youth half lost in his uniform did eventually point me in what appeared to be the right direction. "The matter has been referred to our C.I.D. who are based in Hereford." More cajoling and I managed to elicit the name of the officer in charge of Tom's case – D.C. Winters.

I took the opportunity to do some grocery shopping and snatch a lunch in a supermarket's cafeteria. Being dissatisfied with the latter I was obliged to remind myself that generally one gets what one pays for and I had only myself to blame.

As Tom was not aware that I was on an expedition that morning to fight his cause I did not have any explaining to do when I reached Well Cottage. I pondered a question. If I turned up at Hereford Police Station unannounced what were the chances that I would find D.C. Winters at his desk? I settled on an answer of "not good". Thereby I was prompted to make a telephone call.

"D.C. Withers is a woman," the Administration Officer informed me. "She is attending a course at West Mercia Police H.Q. Be back in the office on Friday. Can I take a message, sir?"

"No thanks, I'll try and catch her then." I cut the line in case I was asked the nature of my business.

Tom came down from his office mid-afternoon to join me for coffee and I told him about my visit to Harcross but not the following one in Leominster. At first he was as puzzled as I was because Christine had not been a member of the church there, despite her mother's certainty that she had been. However, he soon put his finger on what could be an obvious explanation. "You've put your money on the one with the spire, Dad, there could be other churches there. Was she a Methodist, a Jehovah or even a Quaker?"

"Quakers have Meeting Houses and Jehovah Witnesses' Kingdom Halls. But I take you point. I should have thought of that. I suppose that I could telephone Mrs Palmer. She might bite my head off though."

"Why should she? Besides, you and Mum taught us all about sticks and stones and all that."

I did telephone Elizabeth Palmer that evening and her husband answered the phone. I identified myself and at first I thought that he would cut me off. He did eventually condescend to call his wife and she was reasonably affable. "At first Christine was C & E as we had brought her up to be but after a distressing incident with that bastard Rector of St. Edmunds in the village, she became a Baptist. We attended her baptism. What a palaver; not just a sprinkling of water, they bathe in it, full immersion no less."

I drove out to Harcross the following morning. In contrast to the previous day the heavens deigned to produce a steady downpour which very much dimmed the view of St. Ethelbert's as I descended into the valley. The village was not overly large and I was able to drive around most of its street in fairly quick time. There was no sign of the Baptist Church nor, because of the downpour probably, was there anyone to ask.

I sat in the car close to the crossroads for quite some time hoping to alight on a pedestrian who might be braving the weather. Happily I did better than that in the form of a red Post Office van and its postman doing his daily round of deliveries. Of course he knew exactly where I should find the church but his directions ended with the uncompromising comment, "You'll be lucky to find anybody there this time of day."

No wonder I had missed finding the church. At the entrance to an alleyway between two houses, in a row of unremarkable ex-council dwellings, a glass fronted notice board with a faded painted heading declared 'Harcross Baptist Church'. In the box behind the glass were a good number of notices secured by rusty drawing pins and vying with each other for space. The header, curled at the edges and yellowing, advertised the dates and times of services as one would expect. Four postcards offered for sale a lawn mower, a Ford Escort car, a set of baby clothes and gardening services. The paper in the centre caught and held my attention. Advertising a forthcoming trip to a convention in Birmingham the typed document was signed by Pastor William Wright.

"I love pasta." Christine's words not seventy-two hours before. That did not make sense. "I love Pastor" certainly did. I stared at the word long enough to get almost soaked to the skin. I completed that discomfiture by venturing on foot down the narrow drive between the two houses to find a modern church, looking more like a village hall in my eyes, sitting in the centre of a largish plot of land shared with a gravelled car park. I remember thinking that, when they built the church, it must have been a small miracle that heavy builders' merchant's lorries were able to squeeze through from the road.

There were no cars to be seen and I could tell at a glance that the church was almost certainly empty and locked up tight. This did not stop me approaching the double mahogany coloured doors with their large and welcoming glass panels – a stark contrast to the massive and forbidding oak doors of St.

Ethelbert's down the road. Another notice was stuck to one of the panes with cello tape. The signature was a more informal "Bill Wright" and, glory be, his telephone number was there too and I made a mental note of it.

By this time rainwater was leaking into me making me thoroughly uncomfortable. I was wearing my trusty Barbour jacket over a shirt and vest. The manufacturers of Barbour jackets, up there in South Shields, do not claim their garments to be rainproof and certainly not from leaks down the neck and I was bearing testament to that. I stripped off in the car to the waist and wrapped a tartan picnic rug around me and headed straight home. I reasoned that, it being mid-summer, I would be unlucky to develop a chill. Since Angela's untimely and unexpected death I had determined to take care of myself more.

Having revived with a cup of coffee I punched in the Pastor's number on the house phone – or should I say the cottage phone. Bill's voice answered in the form of a recorded message inviting me to state my business and he would contact me. I declined that offer and tried several more times during the day with the same result. At dinner that evening I resisted the urge to tell Tom about my discovery on the grounds that he would more than likely lose no time in sharing the information with Jazz. She did not need any encouragement to set her off on a new crusade.

At nine that night I at last made contact with a living voice but of a woman. "Mrs. Wright?" I ventured.

"Who's speaking please?"

"My name is Desmond Harper. I was hoping to speak to Pastor Wright."

"One moment please. I'll fetch my husband for you."

I imagined she be inured to fielding calls from strangers – some of whom were in trouble and the subject of their call being of a delicate nature. Her few words gave me the impression of her professionalism in that regard.

"Bill Wright, can I help you?" The voice was friendly but measured.

I had planned as to how I would make my approach. "My name's Des Harper and I live not far away from Harcross. I have a problem – it's a bit ticklish – do you hold a surgery or could you spare me a few minutes of your time perhaps, face to face?"

"Are you selling something?" the voice hardened.

"No, no." I realised than my carefully rehearsed approach was not without its flaws. "It's church business – concerning one of your congregation who died some time ago."

"Oh, I see. Can you give me some idea of the nature of your enquiry?"

"It's a bit sensitive really. I would rather talk to you in the flesh as it were. Just an informal chat would do and I won't take up much of your time."

The line went quiet except for some background humming and hawing. "I have to be at the church in Harcross in the morning to supervise some volunteers. I could spare a few minutes if you could find your way there?"

"I visited the church today Pastor, that is how I obtained your number."

"Are you of our faith, Desmond?"

Perhaps my referring to him as "Pastor" had prompted the question. "No, I'm not of any faith."

"Shame; but it's never too late," said the voice dryly. "In the morning then, say about ten-thirty?"

On the strength of that I poured myself a triple whisky which I sipped with Denzil curled on my lap. Tom joined me soon after and we watched television together in relative silence.

"Some volunteers" turned out to be an understatement. The village street around the church's entrance was strewn with parked cars as was much of the car park. The entrance doors were wide open revealing a hive of industry. The rows of chairs that I had seen through the glass the day before were now neatly stacked against walls and replaced by oblong trestle tables which were in various stages of being loaded with wares. Obviously a jumble sale or a summer fete was afoot. I had hardly advanced a few paces inside when a youngish woman detached herself from the melee and approached me with a smile."Hello, a new face, have you come to help?"

"Alas, no," I said. "I've come to see Pastor Wright."

"Bill?"

I nodded. The woman scanned the room and pointed out a rotund middle-aged man in an open collared chequered shirt. "There he is, over there."

As if by telepathy the object of her finger turned in our direction, hesitated, and then made its way over. "Are you the chap who rang me last night?" I nodded and we shook hands. "Follow me." We ended up in a small room hardly big enough for a table and a handful of uncomfortable looking folding chairs. We arranged ourselves opposite each other.

It just occurred to me, however unlikely it may be, that Pastor Bill could have been associated with the Harcross church seventeen years and more earlier and could possibly be the villain that I was searching for. I decided to proceed with caution and not show my hand unwittingly.

"Thanks for seeing me Pastor. Can I ask how long you've been associated with this church in Harcross?

The minister paused for thought. "About six years. Before that my wife and I pursued our calling in Ghana."

"Ghana? I'm impressed."

"We were privileged to share our worship with the good folk of Kumasi. Few people have heard of it. Have you ever been to Ghana, Desmond?

"Alas no. I haven't been to Africa even,"

"Our time there was most rewarding. Now, how can I be of service to you? Or perhaps I should ask how God can help you?"

"You will find my quest to be a little unusual. I live in a cottage in which the daughter of a previous owner was drowned, in a pond that used to be in the garden. I am trying to piece together her story and her mother has informed me that she was a member of the Baptist fellowship and she regularly attended your church here in Harcross .I am hoping to find people who knew her; the Pastor particularly."

The man's face saddened professionally and he took a long pause. "Are we talking Miss Palmer here?" My surprise obviously registered on my face. "Miss Christine Palmer?"

"You know of her?"

"Our congregation at the time felt that they had failed her and as a fellowship we still do. We remember the anniversary of her death in our prayers here every year."

"You never met her, Bill?"

"Of course not – I was in Ghana and never expected to be Pastor here. But there are a number of our Fellowship who do remember our poor daughter."

"Here today? In the church out there?" nodding towards the door.

The man thought for a while. "Give me a minute." He left the room to return with a middle-aged woman in his wake. "This is Margaret. She knew Christine as well as anybody so I believe." The woman was motioned to take a seat.

"Hello Margaret." We shook hands. "I'm Desmond. I live in the cottage where Christine died."

"I didn't know Christine that well. I don't think that any of us did. She was a quiet girl and kept herself to herself for the most part. Her death was a terrible shock. I wouldn't have thought her to be the suicide type. We were all so surprised and saddened, of course."

"You knew that she was three months pregnant?"

"Only because I read a report in the Hereford Times. None of us knew until then."

"She attended church every Sunday?"

"Without fail – except the one time when she was poorly and when she went on holidays of course."

"And she attended week-day classes?"

"Sorry?"

"I have it on good authority that she was attending evening bible reading classes or something similar?"

Margaret looked genuinely confused. "There was nothing regular like that. There never has been as long as I can remember."

"Who was the Pastor here when she died?"

"Pastor McGuire." replied Margaret unhesitatingly.

"You're very sure about that," I observed.

"Angus was really cut up about her death. He tried to soldier on as Pastor here but in the end he retired to somewhere in Inverclyde. That's in Scotland though I'm not sure where."

"He retired? How old was he?"

"I'm not sure. Getting on for seventy I would have thought." A dawning crossed Margaret's eyes. "Were you wondering if Angus could be the father of Christine's baby?" I must have looked slightly embarrassed. "No chance, absolutely no chance. If you had met him you would know immediately." The woman's face coloured in her anxiety to stress the Pastor's innocence.

I didn't ask her to elucidate for fear it could have caused a break in trust between us. "Were there any other Pastors working here in say the six months or so before Christine's death?"

"Are you suggesting that a Pastor was the father of poor Christine's child?" interrupted Bill somewhat fiercely.

"I'm just trying to cover all bases, Jim," I replied lamely with a feeling that my credibility was slipping away.

"Christine had a boyfriend, I know that for sure," waded in Margaret picking up on Bill's indignation. "A boy called Terry. Wasn't he the father?"

"Most likely," I soothed, " I just want to see whom she had any contact with in the last months of her life. She looked to your church for enlightenment and I wanted to know if she had contact with any other Pastors who might have helped her along the road." I never considered myself to be a good liar and I seemed to be proving that point all too well.

Deviousness was lost on the good woman Margaret, much to her credit. She was continuing to bristle and Pastor Bill's body language indicated he had a mind to bring the interview to an end. I needed to head him off.

"Christine held Pastors in great respect. If she was going to confide in anyone her religious leader would be a prime choice, I would have thought."

Providence was seemingly on my side, because the Pastor's mobile sprang into life. Bill rescued the instrument from a breast pocket in his checked shirt, gazed at the number identifying the caller and excused himself. He left the room, in search of privacy I surmised. Grabbing the opportunity that had arisen I turned to Margaret and asked her again, more directly this time, if she could remember the names of other Pastors that might have had contact with Christine.

"As far as I remember we had visits from two Pastors in the year before Christine died. Pastor Neilson came from Sweden and gave a series of talks about the church in Scandinavia as well as some pastoral care. That was open to all our members. Pastor Harris – he was actually just an elder but we often call them pastors when they are employed as teachers. He came and gave a serious of seminars for teenagers; young adults that is. You know," Margaret blushed, "on delicate subjects."

"Sort of sex education?" I asked bluntly.

"Yes, sort of," agreed the woman, reddening more.

"Do you remember where Pastor Harris was based, Margaret?"

The woman thought for some time. "Wolverhampton or Smethwick. He lived in one and attended church in the other – I can't remember which is which."

At that moment Bill Wright re-appeared and stood by the open door expectantly. I guessed this was an urbane way of indicating that my time had expired.

"I don't suppose you know his current whereabouts, Margaret?" I felt that I was onto something and was intent in squeezing out as much information as I could.

"No, we've never seen him since."

"Who are you talking about?" interjected Pastor Wright.

"Pastor Harris. He gave a series of special classes here in Christine's time," the woman answered.

"Special classes?" queried Bill.

Margaret coloured again. "You know – adult topics," she stammered clearly embarrassed.

The Pastor, probably picking up on the woman's unease and to save her any further discomfort, abruptly called a halt to the proceedings. In a gentlemanly way he as good as shoved me out of the main entrance.

I went straight home to Well Cottage – all thought of an excursion to see D.I. Winters banished. I thought that I could be onto something and my euphoria was only dampened when Jasmine arrived from London mid-evening. She argued how spurious my newly acquired information was and just because Pastor Harris gave sex education did not mark him out as person who would engage in extra-marital sex – the antithesis of the teachings of his church. However, Jasmine was impressed by my possible identification of 'pasta' being mistaken for 'pastor' and with that element of my detective work that was at the church in Harcross. Without doubt I had climbed a few rungs in her estimation of me.

Tom was showing increasing eagerness to steer Jasmine away from my kitchen table, Denzil curled on her lap, and to entice her down the garden for some "catching up". A pretty euphemism for nooky no doubt.. I had had a few extra scoops with Sam earlier on, him cider and me red wine, and so I was content to see them depart. But only after Jasmine and I had made a plan as to what we should ask Christine the following night – subject to her deigning to communicate of course.

The next morning I was clearing up the kitchen and thought to throw the cork from the empty wine bottle onto the flagstones. Denzil was sitting, statuesque, on the worktop watching me. He looked haughtily down at the cork and then at me, seemingly to say, "If you want that chased round the kitchen floor then you'd better do it yourself". At that juncture Jazz breezed in.

"I've found him," she beamed.

"Whom," I replied unthinkingly.

"Pastor Harris of course." If she had a tail it would have been wagging wildly. I was literally gobsmacked. Hardly ten o'clock and Jazz had apparently cracked what could have been a major problem. "He is still in the Black Country. First name's Devon and he specialises in sorting out problem juveniles. He's highly rated by all accounts. I have a contact number for him too."

Knowing Jazz – and I was getting to know her quite well – I might have expected that she had already tried to make contact. I urged her not to until we gave ourselves time to plan a way ahead. Later that day a nagging doubt in the back of my mind finally revealed itself. The only man that I had ever met who bore the name 'Devon' had been of Jamaican origin; Afro-Caribbean ethnicity. It was a forename that had yet to find favour with Caucasian parents. If Devon Harris was black then surely he could not have been the father of Christine's baby. She would certainly not have been able to pass the baby off to Terry Hall as being his, as she had apparently attempted to do if Terry were to be believed.

Later that afternoon I caught Tom and Jazz as they returned from a shopping expedition in the Golf. I relayed my concerns to the redhead and left her do any necessary research. "Why have a dog and bark yourself," I reasoned ungraciously. But, sure enough, as we assembled in the caravan that late evening Jazz had chewed at the bone, as it were, and found the answer. "You are a clever old sausage, Des, Pastor Devon Harris is a black man."

Disappointment was registered all round. "Were any other names mentioned?" asked Tom eventually.

"Only a Pastor Neilson. He was from Sweden ," I replied. "I had the impression that he was over here on a sabbatical. Bit far to go to dig him out."

"If he's diggable then I'll find him," muttered Jazz darkly.

That was what I wanted to hear as it took the responsibility from off my shoulders. "Don't forget we agreed that this is the last séance tonight," I warned. "We agreed to destroy the damned telephone afterwards."

Jazz muttered something unintelligible which I guessed to be not in full accordance with my statement.

As eleven o'clock approached we fell silent. The second hand moved achingly slowly. "Would she or wouldn't she?"

"Ring… Ring…"

CHAPTER ELEVEN

Jazz grabbed the handset before I could and I was relegated to the earpiece extension. Tom wasn't even in the game.

"Help me, Help me." I had heard that pathetic opening many times before.

"Where are you?" I heard Jazz ask.

"I'm in the pond. He drowned me and my baby. Help me, help me."

"Who drowned you?" Jazz implored.

"My lover. Help me, help me. My poor baby."

"Is Terry your lover?" asked Jasmine directly.

There was a marked silence broken eventually by the monotonous "Help me."

"Is the Pastor your lover?"

Again a marked silence before, "I love Pastor."

"What's Pastor's name?" asked Jazz urgently.

An even longer silence this time broken by, "He killed me… and my baby… our baby."

And that was it; short and sweet and tantalisingly vague as always. I believe that Jazz and I would have sat there in silence for some time had not Tom pestered us to divulge what we had heard. Jazz filled him in rather ungraciously. "And I'll tell you what Des," she added hotly, "no way am I agreeing to destroy the telephone until we get to the bottom of this. I'll take the bloody thing back to London with me if I have to."

Tom, probably appreciating that there was a chance that he would lose his week-end companion and the comforts that she bestowed on him, was quick to support her.

I threw my hands in the air in an exaggerated gesture of exasperation. "The telephone belongs to me and so I have the final word."

"The phone once belonged to you, Des," was Jazz's quick rejoinder. "You threw it away and now finders keepers applies."

What could I say to that? I really had no answer other than to stomp my way over the grass and up to the cottage with murder in my heart. Denzil was quick to realise that I was upset as I failed to acknowledge him when he attempted to rub against my leg – his usual form of greeting. I brooded over a tumbler of whisky which did little to raise my morale. "I am just going to wash my hands of the whole business," I told myself.

I did my best to avoid both Jasmine and Tom on the Sunday and I rather think that they played the same game with me. I was not about to hold a long term grudge because I was quite a fan of the feisty young lady and I believed her to be an excellence influence on my son. I had made this clear to Tom and he no doubt transmitted this to Jazz during one of their daily chats.

With the plight of Christine Palmer, theoretically at least, consigned to the dustbin, I turned my attention back to the complaint laid against my son by Terry Hall. I drove into Hereford that Monday afternoon, parked in St. Owens Street and walked the short distance to the police station. The civilian desk clerk was surprisingly helpful, confirmed that D.C. Withers was present in the building and would see me. I was ushered into an interview room adjacent to the reception area where I was to cool my heels for a good twenty minutes. For the whole of that time I was acutely aware that I was likely to have been under surveillance from a candid camera discretely positioned high in one corner.

D.I. Withers was a pert young lady dressed in a crisp white blouse and sporting a cheeky bob hairstyle. She allowed me the hint of a smile as an alternative to a handshake and sat down opposite me with a bare desk between us. "How can I help you Mr. Harper?" An innocent enough introduction but with body language that diluted any optimism that I might still have nursed.

I had never intended to tell the full story – who in their right mind would believe a story about a French telephone, unconnected to a telephonic service, being in communication with a woman long dead? I had a form of nebulous alternative in my mind which might have interested a sympathetic listener; Tom and I had 'reason to believe' that Christine's death had not been suicide. I am ashamed to admit I I chickened out and concentrated on a tale that Tom had meant Terry Hall no harm and was deeply sorry for any offence that he had unintentionally given etc. etc.

D.C. Withers heard me out without interruption allowing me sufficient time to run out of steam. "Have you finished Mr. Harper?" I nodded lamely. "I haven't had time to properly process Mr. Hall's complaint. I will try and deal with it soon and, as Tom's father, I can understand your concern. But unless Terry Hall retracts, it is possible that your son's parole will be revoked – almost certainly if the case goes to court."

What could I do other than to thank the officer and slink away?

That evening I acquainted Tom with the details at my abortive attempt to secure his continued freedom. He was suitably grateful possibly because he had a bombshell to deliver. "I'm afraid Dad that you're going to lose me one way or other. "

"How come?"

"If I have to go back to prison of course. If not, I am planning to move back to London. Many of my business contacts are in the city as you know and being isolated here in rural Herefordshire is not ideal. Besides, I have a care for Jazz having to drive here every week-end. We would much prefer to live together 24/7."

I could see the sense in that. I would have done the same if I were in his shoes. "Where will you live – in Jazz's flat? She has flatmates hasn't she?"

"No, Dad, I'm sorting out a place for both of us."

"Where?"

"You'd have found out eventually and I suppose now is as good a time as any. In Putney – Thames-side views over the river."

"That'll cost you a fortune in rent, son."

Tom's face turned a delicate shade of pink. "Actually Dad, I'm buying it."

"What?" I blurted out in real astonishment. "What with? All your assets were confiscated by the court."

Tom's face reddened further. "Well Dad, I haven't been idle all this time I've been living with you. I've made quite a bit of money."

"Enough to buy a flat on the riverside in Putney? Without being able to get a mortgage?"

Tom nodded. "If I do go back to prison then Jazz will live in the property until I am able to join her. I have put the flat in her name just in case the Official Receiver decides to have another bite of my cherry."

I was at a loss for words. I had to admit to a wave of pride that my son had the acumen to turn his financial affairs around in double quick time. Any doubts as to the propriety of the process I shoved to the back of my mind – at least for the meantime. "I will be sorry to see you leave, son, but I completely understand. Let's christen your new home with a drop of whisky shall we?"

The following morning I was drinking coffee and trying to lessen the dull banging in my head when I became aware of Sam's sparse frame silhouetted in the open kitchen doorway. Whilst it was unusual to see Sam at any time during the week apart from Fridays, early on that Tuesday was a surprise. My immediate thought was that he was in some sort of trouble and I beckoned him inside with sympathy already in my heart. I ushered him to sit and he accepted the offer of a cup of tea.

"We needs to get them barrels and casks up from yon cellar. Them's full of lees and going sour. They needs treating ready for the next 'arvest. That lad of yours could 'elp get them up. I knows that 'e's busy a courting that wench of his at the week-ends."

"You have in mind doing it today?"

"Good as any, gaffer. And I've got a bit of spare time. Nice day for washing them out."

How could I deny him? I knew that the old man hated going down into the cellar – although I had yet to understand why – and I guessed that he would manoeuvre the exercise so that he remained topside. I called up to Tom in his office at the head of the stairs and received a cheerful acquiescence , "Give me five, Dad."

I could hear Tom faintly talking on his telephone and five turned into twenty minutes more like. Probably because I was slightly hung-over conversation between Sam and me dwindled down to a few banalities and the old man's attention turned to Denzil who was sitting on the floor close to my legs. He had been fed, groomed himself and was probably planning his day ahead.

"Do you think that that there kitty could pick up my cap?"

said Sam with the sneer that was his custom. With that he took off his filthy headgear and threw it onto the floor between himself and the cat. Denzil took one glance at the missile and was off with a heartfelt meowwwwww. He was a streak of black and white and through the back door into the garden beyond.

"The cat's no fool, Sam. He remembers the last time that you played that trick on him."

"'Appen 'e does," agreed the old man retrieving his headgear, a tight smile on his lips. "'Appen 'e does."

"Besides," I added, "he's no kitten anymore."

True to form Tom and I lugged and humped the barrels up the cellar steps and out through the kitchen door to lower them on the floor of the yard so that they could be washed out. The plastic casks were no problem but even so Sam wangled the work schedule so as he remained on the upper deck – that was until I called him down with such authority that compelled him to oblige.

Of course I had been down into the cellar on scores of occasions, primarily to store and then fetch cider from both the barrels and plastic casks. But I had never really stopped underground long enough to explore the place and for some reason I did so then. Not that there was much to see.

The walls were of ancient bricks, hand-made judging by their irregularity in shape and consistency. I should say that the floor area was about four yards by three and the height a little over six foot under the beams that held up the floor above. There was no window and a rudimentary electricity supply offered illumination from a naked bulb without an offer of a power point.

The floor was covered in a commercial type hessian, donkey's years old, in one yard wide strips. In our activity of removing the barrels the hessian had been rucked up in the centre of the cellar and an iron ring embedded in the floor had become exposed. To help identify its purpose was the reason that I called on Sam's services. The old shepherd descended the cellar steps gingerly, obviously very ill at ease and he fair hobbled the few steps to where I was standing. I pointed out the iron ring to him and he bent down from his waist, clicking his tongue and snorting. At last he straightened as far as his permanently bowed back would allow and pronounced, "'tis for slaughtering the animals I reckon."

"Slaughtering animals?" I repeated incredulously.

"Sheep most like. Ties 'em to the ring so's they can't escape when they cuts their throat."

"But, but," I protested, "there'll be blood everywhere?"

"Naw, they didn't waste the blood in them days. The missus would catch that in a bucket to make black puddings. Besides, them flags are laid on earth and any liquid would disappear down the cracks. They'd swill the floor down afterwards anyhow."

Sam gave me no chance to question him further as he was already legging it up the rickety steps and out of the subterranean ex-slaughterhouse.

I knew about pig benches and the ceremony of slitting the squealing animal's throat as part of a countryman's ceremonial in days of yore but I had never come across stories of dispatching sheep, or any other animal, in what was essentially a domestic cellar. Still, one lives and learns and I had no better explanation to offer at that moment in time.

If ill-fortune comes in threes, as the old adage goes, then perhaps surprises do as well. On Wednesday I received a phone call from Jazz. Immediately I thought that she wished to speak to Tom, that his line was engaged, and she had resorted to get a message to him via me. But no, I was mistaken.

After the sparsest of preliminaries she blurted, "I've found him. Pastor Neilson, Pastor Sven Jurgen Neilson to be exact."

"How did you manage that?" a perfunctory question as my mind was not fully tuned in.

"Dozens of phone calls to church groups up and down the length of Britain," she exaggerated. "Seriously though, it wasn't easy and there was a good deal of luck involved – especially when I tell you the next bit Desmond."

"Go on," I was quickly tuning my brain to catch up.

"I went round to the Swedish Embassy in Marylebone. And I fluttered my eyelashes at a young man behind the reception desk. I had to accept an invitation to lunch – don't tell Tom please – and that afternoon he looked into some confidential files and found a reference to a Sven Jurgen Neilson who was known to their police."

"For what reason?"

"I'm coming to that, Desmond. He was accused of inappropriate relations with an underage girl in Gothenburg . They were both members of a church there – a Baptist church. What do you think to that? It's just got to be our Pastor Neilson surely?"

"Known to the police; what does that mean?"

"According to my source there wasn't sufficient evidence to sustain a prosecution but his name remains on police files. And the records indicate that he moved to the U.K. Of course, the Swedes lost sight of him from there on. But he's just got to be the Neilson that I've found in Canterbury. There can't be too many Sven Jurgen Neilsons and who are Baptists in this world."

"No," I had to agree. "So he's in Canterbury you say?"

"He's based there but is employed as a visiting Pastor for church groups in East Kent, so I am informed by a contact that I made in Manchester."

"Has he a particular role in the church, do you know?"

"He specialises in sorting out the problems of young people. A whole batch of churches have him on their registers and if one of their congregation requires counselling and the like, Neilson is on a panel. He did the same sort of thing in the North-west before moving to Kent about six years ago."

"Did your Manchester contact happen to hint at any impropriety surrounding Neilson when he was there?"

"No, but the bloke was very clipped with his replies. It wasn't as though we were face to face with each other and I could work my charm on him."

"If Neilson has a question mark against his name in Sweden for a sexual offence against a young woman, a girl even, then you may well be onto something Jasmine." My mind was racing to process this new information. "Where do we go from here I wonder?"

"I don't think that there's much point in approaching the police at this stage. The evidence, such as it is, is circumstantial. I intend to go and visit him and see what transpires from there."

"No, no, Jazz," I exploded in alarm. "You mustn't do that. You could be putting yourself in all manner of danger." I knew how headstrong the girl was and needed to come up with a compromise that would slow her down. "Let's talk about a way forward this week-end."

Jazz went quiet and then said, "I'm a big girl. I can handle this."

"No Jazz," I fair yelled at her. "For once in your life do as you're fucking told."

The vehemence of my outburst seemed, thank goodness, to have an ameliorating effect. I will never know what crashed through her mind but she did rather timidly agree to hold off until after the week-end at least. "Thank God for that." What was I doing thanking a deity that I didn't believe in?

A few minutes after I had replaced the receiver I heard Tom's phone ringing up the stairs. Although he was usually fielding calls throughout the day I just had the thought that particular summons was from his girlfriend. So what if it were…?

I sat sunning myself for a good while in the orchard that afternoon, my mind never far from Sven Neilson and how best to approach the problem that surrounded him. Whatever I came up with it needed to be sound enough to convince the adroit Jasmine. There was no doubt that she was determined not to give up the chase and I felt almost a paternal urge to protect her. If Neilson had drowned Christine Palmer there was no saying what he might be capable of in order to protect his liberty.

I heard a woodpecker tap, tap tapping away somewhere in the distance. Mine was not the only orchard in the vicinity and on a hot, still sunny afternoon noise travelled a fair distance. Sam's forecasting of a bumper harvest had proved correct as most of my apple trees were burgeoning with fruit. Even the oldest trees, losing their fight with parasitical mistletoe, were gamely trying to support the forthcoming autumn harvest. The sward would need cutting again soon. I promised myself to research getting some sheep for next year. That thought brought me back to my cellar being used as an abattoir.

There would be no Peter to help with cider making this coming season. Pictures of him in a range of guises loomed into my brain. Why were they so misty so soon? And I couldn't even remember the name of his last lady friend. Of course, if I hadn't met Peter in the Dog and Duck then I wouldn't have visited France, bought the telephone and my life would have taken an entirely different course – and probably Peter would be alive now. Still, another path could have been considerably worse…

Denzil found me and deigned to keep me company by stretching out on the grass close to my feet. I admired his black and white "Felix" colourings yet again. I invited him to come sit on my lap and I could see him considering the proposition

– and then declining by flopping his head back onto the grass and resuming his original posture.

Over the hedge I could see the top of Tom's caravan. What would he do with that now his plans were to move back to London? If it remained I would have extra dormitory space for visitors. There again, I did not expect to have many guests and I would be able to repossess Tom's office anyway. Perhaps I could offer the caravan as a holiday let and earn some income. Why would I want the hassle? I had enough money to see me off the planet anyway. The few premature apples on the ground were receiving the attention of wasps. Wasps have never worried me – I do not wave my arms like a demented windmill when one appears to take a passing interest in me.

I still didn't know quite what to make of Tom. He was a whiz kid – no doubt about that. And, sure enough, he had paid the penalty for bending the rules. Was he at it again? I dared not ask him, suspecting that he would make denials whatever the reality. My instincts were, however, that Tom was playing by the rules and benefitting from having contacts in the right places. "Insider trading" lurked in the back of my mind and Tom must certainly be gaining some information to substantiate his investment decisions. On the other hand Tom and Jasmine were undoubtedly very fond of each other and the future of that relationship probably depended on Tom not returning to prison for a second, and longer stretch.

The well over in the corner was a bit of an enigma. No doubt located in the lowest part of my land in order to reach the underground water with the least amount of digging out, but it was quite away from the kitchen door. I pitied the poor housewife that needed a supply on inclement days.

By the time that I folded my chair and made my way back up to the cottage I had the embryo of a plan that might satisfy Jazz and move things foreword.

CHAPTER TWELVE

Sunday evening saw me flying down the A419 via Cirencester to the M4 and ultimately West London in a bright red Golf GT1 driven dementedly. At least that was my take on Jazz's driving.

I was dropped off at a Premier Inn close to Jazz's flat with her apologies ringing in my ears. "I am sorry that I can't put you up for the night Desmond, but all my flatmates will be in their beds tonight and I don't think the sofa will suit you. Still, next time we should be able to offer you the luxurious accommodation of a riverside apartment," she added mischievously.

How she and Tom had managed to obtain an interview with Pastor Neilson at such short notice was, in my opinion, nothing short of a miracle. Evidently his Canterbury headquarters, like the Samaritans, operated a twenty-four hour service and had been convinced as to the urgency of a plea from Tom masquerading as being Jazz's father. I hate to think of the number of falsehoods that he had told but then, after all, telling fibs was certainly one of Tom's talents. I consoled myself by a "needs must" justification.

The next day we were somewhere in South London when a thought struck me. "I forgot to ask Jazz. Did the telephone ring on Saturday night?" In my guise of washing my hands of the instrument I had declined the offer to attend the caravan.

"Sure thing, bang on time."

"And?"

"Same as before. Nothing new. Christine declined to answer any of my questions. Very frustrating."

Our appointment was for 2.30 pm on the Monday at a venue in Folkestone, that location being the only condition necessary if we insisted on seeing Pastor Neilson and not another counsellor on the panel. Traffic held the Golf's speedometer in check until we achieved the M20 where I made a condition of my co-operation that we stayed within the 70 mph speed limit.

With plenty of time to waste I suggested that I treat Jazz to a lunch at The Grand on The Leas, central Folkestone. We sat in the plush conservatory overlooking the English Chanel and enjoyed an excellent meal spoilt only because we both needed to abstain from alcohol, and wine in particular. We both needed clear heads notwithstanding that Jazz would be driving us back to London later in the day.

I had expected our interview venue to be attached to a Baptist church and not what was once a shop in a modest area, its large window swathed in vertical blinds. The frontage was totally anonymous except for a prominent door bell incorporating a 24-hour illumination and a circular Yale lock. I have to admit that my hand was trembling as I announced our presence by pressing the bell.

The odds that the figure who opened the door were at least a thousand to one that he wasn't a Swede, or at least a Scandinavian. The archetypal blonde hair neatly groomed, faraway deep blue eyes and a tall lithe figure were a near certainty. He was dressed in a checked shirt, lumberjack style with short cream shorts that emphasised his genital bulge. A fact that I felt would not be lost on Jasmine. Tanned face, arms and legs completed the ensemble. No way did he look fortyish in years and he was not at all what I envisaged a Pastor in the Baptist Church to be.

He introduced himself as "Pastor Sven" with eyes that gave preference to Jasmine – I received little more than a glance. The set-up of the room immediately inside the front door has been prepared with three comfortable leather chairs arranged round a coffee table. Other chairs were tucked away to one side. Apart from a modern sideboard there was no other furniture and no pictures. Minimalistic would be an apt description although the carpet was plush and the room cool albeit the day was warm outside.

"So you will be Jasmine?" opened the Pastor when we were all comfortably seated. I was grateful that apparently I wasn't going to have to lie about my name and role. "And you work in London?"

"I'm here under false pretences, Pastor. It is you that I particular want to meet." She looked across at me. "And this is Desmond, my future father-in-law."

I winced, wondering if there could be any truth in that.

The Swede's smile dampened quite sharply. "False pretences, Jasmine, that sounds intriguing."

"We're investigating the death of Christine Palmer."

That killed the smile stone death before the man could attempt a quick recovery. "Christine Palmer?"

This approach was not what Jazz and I had agreed beforehand. We had absolutely no proof that Sven Neilson had harmed Christine in any way, or had anything other than a professional relationship, or even had ever met her. The plan was to have softly asked questions aimed at gently drawing the man out and eliminating him as a suspect should that have seemed likely. Instead Jazz had seemingly taken matters upon herself to mount a full frontal attack.

"The name doesn't register with me," added the man after a suitable lapse in time.

Looking to interpret the slightest facial expressions, I wasn't convinced that he was telling the truth.

"You will have met her when you worked at the Baptist church in Harcroft in Herefordshire," prompted Jazz.

"Harcross," I corrected her.

"Harcross? Harcross. " Another long pause. "I did some work in Herefordshire but that was a very long time ago."

"Something like twenty years ago?" offered the girl.

"Look, I've taught and counselled hundreds and hundreds of people since then. I can't be expected to remember all their names." The man was starting to get his confidence back. "Who exactly are you? You're obviously not the police or you would have identified yourselves."

"No," answered Jasmine quickly, "we're not the police but private investigators."

I gulped away the denial on my lips. I caught myself with a thought that technically that was true. My palms were clammy with sweat.

"And who are you working for?" asked the man.

"Mrs. Elizabeth Palmer, Christine's mother," Jazz replied as confidently as if it were true. "You took a series of seminars which Christine attended. She was impressed by you."

"I don't wish to appear immodest," Sven smiled, his confidence mounting again, "but I did have my admirers when I was younger. Of course there was no impropriety. I was very careful on that score."

"Is that right, Mr. Neilson? We have a statement that says that you had a clandestine affair with Christine Palmer."

What a bombshell. Both Neilson and I were visibly startled. Jazz was playing a very dangerous game. I could see the both of us being thrown out into the street in double quick time, but I held my nerve and stared at Neilson full in the face. Not that he noticed as his eyes were fixed on Jazz. He looked like a man who was thinking fast. His smile was more of a grimace. "And who has made that accusation?"

"Christine herself," Jazz lied without blinking an eye."She said that you were the father of her baby."

Jazz's tactics seemed to be to keep up the momentum and thereby denying her opponent much time to think. This was a high risk strategy especially so as we had only the flimsiest indication that Neilson was the father of Christine's baby. All our so-called evidence was circumstantial.

Similar thoughts were possibly in Neilson's mind when he replied. "How on earth can I prove to you that I am totally innocent?"

"By giving us a D.N.A sample Mr. Neilson."

"D.N.A., what's that?"

"I don't know what the acronym stands for but DNA profiling is a method of proving parentage and whether people are related. In your case it could be used to prove that you were not the father of Christine's baby."

"This girl that I have never heard of was pregnant and you suspect that I am the father of her baby?"

I started to wobble. Neilson seemed righteously indignant. I was ready to break the interview up and beat a hasty retreat.

"That is something we should rule out Mr. Neilson. We have the baby's DNA for comparison of course. All we need is a sample from you and, if things are as you say, you will have nothing to fear."

"Nothing to fear?" repeated the man, now visibly agitated. "Even if I were the father of this .. er … woman's baby what would I have to fear?"

"There is compelling evidence that Christine Palmer was murdered."

"Murdered?" Neilson's voice was not far short of a shriek and his face, I swear, appeared to turn white under his tan.

"Yes," replied Jazz calmly. "She was drowned."

Neilson sat silent and then started to say something and decided against. For my part I felt the need to intervene but was completely out of ideas.

"We can clear this whole thing up right now. Agree to give us a blood sample, please," asked Jazz quietly.

"I can't give you one here and now," Sven protested.

"Why not? There is a clinic here in Folkestone that will take a sample of your blood professionally and quickly. I have arranged with them for an open ended appointment and you won't have to wait. You'll be back here in less than thirty minutes."

Neilson was again slow to answer. "I can't spare the time right now," he said defensively.

"Not even to prove your innocence?"

"Why should I need to do that? I have never, ever misbehaved with any of my clients."

"Well, that's not strictly true, is it Mr. Neilson?"

"What are you trying to say?" Neilson half rose in his seat, his face full of indignation.

"My information is that you remain on police files in Sweden for committing a sexual offence," said Jazz blandly.

Neilson lurched back into his chair obviously astounded by the revelation."How the fucking hell did you know that?"

I marvelled as to how urbanity and confidence could so quickly dissipate. What Jasmine came out with next pretty well floored me. "I take it that your Church is aware of your … shady past?"

"Out," shouted the Swede, his face turning red. "Out, get the fucking hell out of here." He stood up. "Both of you, out this minute." Strangely he now looked all of his forty-odd years.

Jasmine and I rose in unison. "I take it you're declining to offer us a blood sample today?" questioned Jazz calmly.

"Out, fucking out."

We had no option to oblige. I would have scarpered but Jazz appeared unfazed and left the building with dignity. On the street the door slammed shut behind us.

Once a safe distance away I turned on my companion. "You've just about broken every rule in the book – stepped way out of line. If Neilson is innocent you've been … cruel." I emphasised the last word almost to shouting point.

Jazz turned to look me straight in the eyes. "He's guilty, Des, have no fear about that," she said calmly and with undeniable conviction.

"How can you be SO sure? There is no evidence whatsoever and you've told a mountain of lies."

"Sometimes the end justifies the means."

"But if he IS innocent then he didn't deserve to have his past dug up like that."

"Why not? If he interfered with an underage girl in Sweden – and the Swedish police are absolutely sure that he did – then he deserves what I gave him."

"And you would rat on him to his Church authorities?"

"If it were a justifiable means to an end, yes. The trouble with you Des is that you are too soft. When it comes to pulling the trigger you just haven't the bottle to do it. Tom has, I'm pleased to say."

That jibe hit home and I smarted."I am not sure that I would want to live in the world you live in," I replied in retaliation.

"No, I don't blame you, you wouldn't survive for long."

The drive back into London need not have been the silent affair that it turned out to be. After all, the experience of the afternoon had left me with more than a sneaking regard for my feisty driver. If I hadn't been a participant but rather a distant observer she would have won my open admiration.

The problem was that I was still far from convinced that we had not frightened an innocent man.

Jasmine dropped me off outside Paddington Station where I was disappointed to find that I had missed a direct train to Hereford and was obliged to take the one to Swansea and change at Cardiff. Happily Tom was sitting in my car at Hereford waiting to give me a lift back to Well Cottage.

Tom was not the loving son that I had become used to these past few months. Jasmine had obviously contacted him whilst I was on route that evening and told him about the events of the day including the strong words that we had exchanged. I had neither made it clear to Jazz that there was nothing personal in my remarks and nor had I demonstrated the admiration that I clearly felt for her. Red haired Jazz, I was to learn, was a woman capable of holding a grudge and Tom was in no doubt as to which side he was on. I didn't blame him for that – I would have done the same in his shoes.

To be fair to Tom, we did largely clear the air between us but neither of us was in any doubt that I would have to work hard to turn Jasmine around. At least Denzil was pleased to see me when I at last stepped through my kitchen door – and that was not because he needed feeding.

Perhaps I might have expected Tom to announce mid-week that there was to be a change of plan. Instead of Jasmine making the pilgrimage to Well Cottage that coming week-end as per usual, Tom was to visit her flat in London on the same basis

And the next two week-ends followed the same pattern, Tom week-ending in London. A move into their new apartment was imminent and soon I would see little of my son – much like my daughter in Australia. All this time there had been no word from the police in Hereford about the complaint hanging over Tom's head. A condition of his parole from prison was that he had to notify the police of his change of address – and that had to be within the U.K. I was concerned that by doing so he could bring adverse attention to himself. Jasmine would say that I was worrying needlessly – again.

Of course I did try to wheedle out of Tom what might Jazz be up to regarding chasing Sven Neilson – or anyone else for that matter. Goodness knows where she might have taken things. No joy at all; Tom proclaimed innocence and again took the road of least resistance. The truth was if I never heard the name 'Christine Palmer' ever again I would have been happy.

Sam had cleaned out and sterilised all the barrels and plastic casks ready for the coming cider-making season. Second time round the ex-whisky barrels would hardly have enough evidence of their past to flavour their new contents. That would be a shame because the added flavour on last season's making greatly enhanced the quality of the cider. I did consider adding a half bottle to each of the barrels when the time came but the idea received no more than a sneer from Sam. "T'aint what we do in 'erefordshire."

For three week-ends the caravan was empty as Tom was away down in London. I ensured that it was locked and, although I had a key, I did not wander down the garden on Saturday nights to see if Christine was still operating, as it were. Perhaps I should have taken the opportunity to go inside and remove the French telephone and dispose of it forever. I was mindful of Jazz's declaration that "finders were keepers" and I chose not to risk antagonising the girl further.

On the fourth week Tom moved out permanently to Putney and reported that they were delighted with their new home. Those were actually Jazz's words to me – we had a telephone conversation that left me encouraged that the pipe of peace was ready for smoking. Hurrah.

I had another telephone call soon after – one that set me back on my haunches even more.

"Mr. Harper?"

"Yes."

"Bill Williams."

"The names familiar but…?"

"Pastor at Harcross. You came to see me several months ago."

"Yes, I remember."

"I would like to talk to you face to face. Is it possible…?"

"That I come to you?" I filled in.

"That would be great." We arranged a time, the next day, for a meeting in the Baptist church in Harcross where we had last met. I had the feeling something of significance was about to come to light – or was it a foreboding?

I knew the route to Harcross of course and the alleyway that led to the Baptist church. Bill Williams was casually dressed as he had been on my last visit but his was not a welcoming smile that in any way matched mine. "Come in the back here," he said showing me into the room as before. "Can I call you Desmond?"

"Of course." We sat down opposite each other.

"You came here some months ago asking about Christine Palmer." I nodded my confirmation. "Her name has come up again – unexpectedly. I feel that I ought to tell you what I have learned."

"Please do."

"A Canterbury office, part of our church, have written to me telling of the sad death of one of their team." I felt something akin to a stab in my side. I guessed straight away whom we were talking about. "Pastor Sven Neilson – have you heard of him?"

"Yes," I answered quietly. "Met him actually."

Bill Williams raised his eyebrows. "Met him?"

"Tell me what you have to say first please Bill."

"Pastor Neilson took his own life a little while back."

The stabbing pain changed to an icy thrill through the whole of my body. I had "I'm sorry to hear that," on my lips but no such utterance left my mouth. Just "Oh."

"He left a note; more of a confession really. He wrote that he needed to meet his maker having confessed his sins. We in the church would expect no less in the circumstances. Especially from a Pastor."

"Yes, I suppose so."

"He wrote confessing that he was responsible for making your Christine Palmer pregnant. And for drowning her in the pond at Well Cottage. There were other misdemeanours evidently but I am not privy to those – only to that one that affects the church here. We will, of course, mention Pastor Neilson in our prayers."

"And Christine Palmer too?" I said tersely with a smell of hypocrisy drifting across my nose.

"Oh, yes, of course, poor Christine too," replied the Pastor hastily.

I drove out of Harcross a very, very relieved man. And I felt a stone lighter too – that great weight gone from my shoulders. And, fuck me, that little shrew Jasmine had been right all along. Full credit to her. Cor, she'll make Tom an excellent wife. Fuck me. Did I feel sorry that Pastor Sven Neilson had taken his own life? Not a bit did I. I gave him credit though for having made a full confession. Christine and her baby could now rest in peace.

CHAPTER THIRTEEN

Once I had recovered my equilibrium and euphoria that justice of sorts had been achieved for poor Christine Palmer my thoughts focused on her mother, and to some degree her father too. They were undoubtedly first on my list of "need to know".

My knee jerk reaction was to telephone Elizabeth Palmer but after careful consideration I decided that I could not trust myself to achieve the right level of euphoria, or perhaps gravitas. Goodness knows how the conversation might have been. Much the same applied to a personal visit. A letter became my preferred medium and I wrote accordingly.

I did the same with Jasmine but for entirely different reasons of course. I wanted to put her in no long lasting doubt that she was fully responsible for having achieved such a positive outcome. If it weren't for her, and her alone, there would have been no justice for Christine Palmer and no closure for her parents. I told her that I admired her courage, resolve and fortitude. I unconditionally heaped praise on her. And I meant every word of it.

Whilst those two letters were winging their way there was a third necessity in my head. I drove into Hereford and bought a bottle of decent whisky, a tray of quality beers and an expensive bouquet of flowers. My next call, early evening, was to a house in Kington where, armed with my booty, I knocked on a shabby front door. I noticed the resulting twitch in the dirty net curtains in a window immediately to the left.

The woman who answered to door somewhat reluctantly was formidable, in size, in shape and in facial expression. Her perfume was tobacco and her jewellery a brown elastic band pulling her brown hair into a tight pony tail; the sort the Post Office use. I glimpsed a man standing in the back of the hall and I imagined that this was a practised campaign position against debt collectors and the like. I introduced myself and the woman's face turned slightly from aggressive to blank. Disclosing that I was Tom's father engendered close to a war cry. The flowers probably saved my bacon.

I related as best as I could that Christine's death had been resolved and that Terry had been exonerated both from the accusation that he was the father of Christine's baby and for her death. The further that I explained the history, the nearer Terry approached from the back of the hall until he was standing right behind his partner (she may have been his legal wife for all I knew). I could see that Terry became increasingly relieved but the woman's face hardly changed at all. Fancy living with that on a day to day basis.

I offered the presents and Terry would have pushed forward to grab the liquids at least. Grumpy stopped him and demanded to know "the catch. Nobody gives us nowt for nuffink round here, mate."

"There's no catch, they are a present from my son Tom for annoying you when he visited you. He was just trying to get to the truth about Christine and he's achieved that. Bothering you was just part of the investigation process. Aren't you glad Terry to learn the truth and be entirely in the clear?"

Terry nodded, his eyes hardly straying from the booze in my arms. "I sure am," he said magnanimously.

"Would you withdraw the complaint you made to the police?" A risky question that just had to be asked. "Please."

"Depends," said the wolverine moving her plump body a shade to prohibit Terry's access to my goodies.

Negotiations were brisk and I left with my wallet bereft of the fifty pounds that I held as a banker. "Cheap at the price," I grinned to myself. Providing of course that they contact the police in the morning as they promised to.

Elizabeth Palmer telephoned me with my letter fresh out of its envelope. I heard snatches of crying in the background which I suspected was her husband, "How can I thank you Des, etc. etc. etc."

Unabashed I took the credit rightly attributable to Jasmine. "Keep things simple," I told myself. There was no doubt that my news had been a tremendous comfort and relief to the Palmers. Good old Jazz.

Tom had had his mail redirected on his removal to Putney – much to the delight of my permanent postman I suspect. He was overwhelmed both by a number of "sign fors" every week notwithstanding the quantity of large envelopes he was obliged try to stuff through my letter box. The letter from the police went straight to Tom. He rang me and told me in a matter of fact attitude that Terry Hall's complaint had been withdrawn. I didn't tell him that it had cost me a great deal of angst as well as fifty pounds and an armful of other bribes. But that is what Dad's do isn't it?

About that time I returned from shopping in Leominster to find Interflora had left a huge bouquet of flowers in my front porch. They must have cost a small fortune and I had absolutely no idea as to who they might have been from. That was certainly not my son's modus operandi. The card read "From Elizabeth Palmer. I can't thank you enough. God Bless." As big and old as I am I could not help shedding a tear or two.

For the first time in months I felt almost totally relaxed; happy even. I might have known that this euphoria was merely the peace before the storm.

We were into September when Tom telephoned me to say, quite casually, that he and Jazz intended to pop in and see me that coming Saturday. Would I be at home? No, they didn't want to stay the night because they were off to attend a concert at Aberystwyth University that Saturday evening but they wouldn't decline lunch. I was very pleased and looked forward to hearing all their news.

I mowed the orchard for the last time before the apple harvest and felt guilty watching the sit-on spewing out shredded apple as I had not bothered to rake up the relatively few fallen earlies. I tried to console myself by thinking that most would not have been suitable for cider making anyway. Against that they could have made suitable pig food. Old habits die hard. Although I was wealthy in terms of the population in general, the relative poverty that beset my parents when I was a child has instilled in me an undeniable parsimony.

As I moved on to cut the grass of the back lawn the problem of the future of Tom's caravan could not fail to arrest me – being as the structure was right there in my face. I resolved to bring up the subject come Saturday. The heavens were kind because the rain held off right to the moment that I had safely stashed the sit-on in the garage. Then it came down in buckets for the following twenty-four hours.

Sam turned up true to form on the Friday and we had a few "harns" together. The old shepherd was grateful that the bought-in keg of cloudy draught was located in the kitchen's pantry rather than down in the cellar. We discussed the amount of rain that had fallen – and was still falling – the bumper apple harvest and inevitably, our plans for cider making the following month. We decided not to repeat the Yarlington Mill and Ten Commandments experiment and instead be content with one grand mix – all in the mill together. Even the world weary Sam showed a modicum of emotion when we discussed the fact that there wouldn't be Peter to help us this time.

Denzil was wary of Sam – quite rightly so I suppose. There was no rubbing himself against the old shepherd's leg and certainly no attempt to jump onto his lap. At one point I asked Sam a question and apparently the answer required him to lift his cap and scratch the fore part of his head. The hand to the cap sent Denzil scurrying out of the kitchen…

When Sam started wheezing and sniffing we both knew the signs that it was time for him to go. To his home? Probably not – rather a couple more pints with his mates down the Tap Room of the Dog and Duck. "You want to see old Percy. Last week 'e came in and 'is face was as yella as the cider. Still is. We 'ad a good laugh about it." I was not at all surprised that Percy was dead soon after from liver failure. Mind you he was nearly eighty and had had a good innings.

Saturday morning dawned and I felt elated at the thought of seeing Tom and Jazz. I prepared toad-in-the-hole, boiled potatoes and garden peas which used to be Tom's favourite. I had a salad handy too, just in case Jasmine was having a figure conscious day. At first I had thought that she was one of those lucky young women who enjoyed a keen appetite and yet maintained an enviable trimness, before Tom let slip her regular attendance at a gymnasium. To me that was a generational thing.

Soon after eleven o'clock I hear what only could be Jazz's Golf GTI vrooming in through the front gates. I went out to meet them, umbrella at the ready because the rain had not eased. I went to kiss Jazz perfunctorily on both cheeks but she drew right into me and added a huge hug. All was now sweet between us, no doubts about that. That gave me an added boost of pleasure. Tom looked well as did Jazz. Obviously their living together was beneficial to both of them.

We sat down at the kitchen table and drank coffee. The kitchen was the place to be, especially as I had turned up the Aga to make the kitchen snug as an antidote to the relentless rain outside. Jazz seemed delighted still to be the centre of Denzil's attention as the cat would settle for nothing less that laze on her lap. Once we had exhausted the preliminaries I raised the question of the caravan whilst it was still in the forefront of my mind.

"You can have the caravan as a present if you want. It would be handy if you had lots of people to stay. Or you could sell the van and keep the money as sort of delayed rent for when I was here. It probably would fetch not too far short of a five figure sum."

"That's very kind of you, son," I replied, bemused that he could write off so much money so impassively. "If I do sell then I will give you the money to buy stuff for your new flat."

"Apartment," interjected Jazz laughing.

"Oh, yes." I smiled back. "Nothing so common as a flat for you two."

"We'll borrow umbrellas and go and pack up the last of my few things left in there, if that's O.K. with you." said Tom. "There's not much, just a few papers and books really."

"And that fucking telephone." I had forgotten all about that. "We must get rid for good and all."

I caught Jazz and Tom exchanging glances. "Ah," said the girl, "we need to talk about that but let's have lunch first."

That sounded ominous but I let it go for then. But I knew that there was something brewing that I probably wasn't going to like at all.

Whilst my guests were down in the caravan and stuffing black bin bags into the Golf I prepared lunch and laid the table. Denzil would have followed his heroine had it not been for the weather and was obliged to content himself guarding the kitchen door to await Jazz's return. I had a bottle of red wine breathing on the dresser and cans of soft drinks with Jazz in mind. The actuality became that Jazz shared the wine with me and Tom chose plain tap water.

"That's the deal," said Jazz, "I drove from London and Tom drives to Wales."

During the cheese board I said, "Come on, spoil my day and spill the beans. Where is the telephone?"

Jazz looked decidedly uncomfortable. "The simple answer to that Des, is the 'phone's in Putney, in the apartment, and has been so since Tom moved out. He brought it with him on my asking. I am totally to blame for that."

"You knew how much I wanted it destroyed?"

"I do. But I wanted to see out the Christine affair – particularly after our visit to Folkestone that day. You may have thought that I was very single minded, very positive during the interview but I really didn't know where that came from. And afterwards I didn't quite know what to do next. Neilson's suicide came as a shock to all of us. If he hadn't topped himself I really don't think that we'd have ever got a result."

"O.K., so you kept the 'phone just in case Christine came through with some better information?"

"Exactly Des."

"It's academic now, but did she?"

"No, she didn't. The same mantra as before."

"So that's the end of the matter and we can destroy the instrument?"

Jazz coloured and became increasingly nervous. "Of course, we learned about Neilson's suicide some weeks after the actual event. Working backwards Christine's last contact coincided as near as dammit with Neilson's suicide ."

"That makes sense," I interrupted. "The same happened when the bomb exploded and the pilot stopped coming through."

"Yes, but the telephone hasn't stopped ringing – just a different time and," she hesitated and took a gulp of air, "a different voice."

"What?" I shrieked.

"Steady on Dad, you'll do yourself some harm," said Tom trying to cool the temperature.

"But don't you see what this means the two of you? Your flat – your apartment – is likely to be tainted. These voices relate to places. Christine was murdered in the very garden outside. The French people who sold me the 'phone possibly lived nearby the crash site. These things are locally related – I am sure of that."

"You may well be right, Des," answered Jazz unhappily. "You won't like what I am about to say. Almost certainly these new messages started when the telephone was still in the caravan here at Well Cottage."

"How do you work that out?"

"Jazz and I have worked it out, over and over," said Tom taking over. "We are positive that the new voice started when the 'phone was in the empty caravan. They no longer come late on a Saturday night. So far the damn thing rings on a Tuesday, at a quarter past two in the afternoon. The caravan was empty and it is unlikely that you would have heard the ringing unless you happened to be standing close outside. We are only wise to it because Tom works from home, in the flat – I mean – apartment."

"Besides, the poor guy would hardly be down a well under the apartments in Putney," added Jasmine. "The builders would have surely come across such a structure when they dug out for our underground car park."

"A well, did you say?" I exclaimed horrified.

"Oh dear. Jazz and I thought very hard before deciding to tell you. I'm not at all sure now that we have done the right thing." Tom looked visibly contrite.

"You have and the damage is done. You had better finish what you have started and tell me what the voice said."

"He doesn't say that much really. Jazz has been at work every time so I am the only one to hear him. The usual 'Help, Help,' is followed by 'I'm down the well' and 'Get me out, get me out'. I have tried asking questions – his name and how did he get there and such like – but I'm given no answer. Christine was much more forthcoming and, from what you have told me, the pilot was a veritable chatterbox."

I fell into a long silence – one that neither Jasmine nor Tom seemed willing to break.

"So, where's the telephone now? Have you brought it back here with you?"

"We thought about doing that," said Tom. "We literally tossed a coin and tails said to leave it in London."

"Maybe just as well," I answered after some consideration. "I would have probably have gotten the sledge hammer to it, the way I feel at this moment."

"There is a well here at the cottage, isn't there Des?" asked Jazz unhelpfully.

"Yes, in the bottom corner of the orchard, near the field gate leading into the lane."

"I haven't noticed one before," she continued.

"It's not surrounded by pretty red bricks, a tiled canopy and a twee pail in fancy rope," I replied sarcastically.

"Then what does it look like above ground?" asked the girl unfazed

"There are a couple of large concrete paving slabs at ground level – easy to miss."

"And undisturbed?"

"Yes. They don't look as though they have been moved in donkey's years. I wouldn't have known that there was a well underneath except that Sam told me when we were cider making nearby last Autumn."

"So, if there were somebody down the well we are not talking recently?"

"I should think not."

"How deep is it?"

"How the fuck should I know, Jasmine," I retorted testily.

"Sam might have told you replied," the girl replied huffily.

"I'm sorry to bark at you Jazz. This has come as quite a shock. If only I hadn't met Peter in the pub that night he would still be alive and I wouldn't be having any of this angst."

"And Sven Neilson would be walking free and Christine Palmer unavenged," added Jazz quickly.

"There's no flies on you, is there?" I commented approvingly.

"The question remains, what are we going to do about the man in the well?"

"We? Where does 'we' come into this, Jazz?"

"After Christine I have developed a taste for this type of posthumous investigative work."

"I need to think this over. You can see that I am in shock, of sorts. If I need you I shall certainly look to employ your proven skills."

"Be sure that you do, Des," said Jazz reassuringly. "I'll give you all the help I can and I'm sure that Tom will too."

"That goes without saying of course Dad," added Tom rising from the table. "I think that we ought to get going now as Wales is calling."

"Can't we nip down and see this well before we go?" asked Jasmine eagerly.

"In that rain Jazz" I pointed to the glass in the kitchen door. She would have been down the garden, umbrella in hand had Tom and I allowed her to.

It being Saturday Sam called in as was his routine and he caught me deep in thought. I had hardly moved from the kitchen chair since my visitors had departed nor had I paid much attention to the cat sitting on my knee. "Evening Gaffer," he said even though it was hardly five o'clock. I found myself wondering at what time the afternoon ended and evening started.

"Just the very man," I replied. Sam's face brightened. Those few words meant there were possibilities and any help that he could render would almost certainly be rewarded by more than a drop of the yellow stuff. "The well in the orchard. I want you to tell me all you know about it."

Sam licked his lips deliberately to signal that his tongue could be best loosened with a drop of cider. I read the message loud and clear and made for the pantry, returning with a full jug. Meanwhile Sam retrieved two glasses from off the dresser.

"That there well was sunk about the time I was born, so my Pa told me. It's way down in the orchard 'cos them what live here were mean buggers. The lower down it was, the shorter it was to dig down to the water, and cost less."

"That makes economic sense," I encouraged.

"I remember that it had a bucket, and a pail and a winding gear and a rusty old corrugated iron shelter on top. They reckoned 'twas sweet water."

"Go on,"

"When the 'lectric came, soon after, the people what lived here then, put in a pump so as I remember. Did away with the pail and stuff and put stones on top. Don't think they have ever been moved since. Next people had the mains water piped in and the well weren't needed no more."

"So the top's not been off that well for thirty years or more?"

"More'n'like. You thinking of using it again Gaffer? Save on the water bills?"

I laughed. "There's a thought now. May be worth finding out if the water's still as sweet as you say?"

Sam screwed up his nose in a classic non-reply mode. "We ain't on a meter 'ere. What's to gain from doing that?"

"Might make better cider," I replied with a flash of inspiration.

Sam thought that idea over. "'appen it might," he conceded finally.

"If it's stopped raining tomorrow perhaps you could call round and we'll try and test the water?"

"'appen I might," said Sam, confidently reaching for the jug of cider on the table before us.

CHAPTER FOURTEEN

I could hardly sleep that night. The premature and traumatic death of my dear wife and confidante, Angela , was too far back in history for mourning on a daily basis or even weekly, but that night I missed her dreadfully. What would I have given to be able to cling to her and lay my head on her soft, scented breast? Unusually I felt alone in the world – apart from the gremlins nibbling at my brain.

What the fuck had I done to deserve all this angst? The bomb episode was bad, very bad, but the Christine saga was even worse in its way. And now I had a third bombardment of evil – that is exactly what it felt like as I lay in that darkened bedroom. I wanted to leave, to sell up, to escape and relocate somewhere very, very far away. Woe was me.

The dawn chorus cheered me up somewhat as I told myself that at least I was still above the turf rather than in a grave below. Denzil rarely slept on my bed but there he was curled into a ball until he saw my legs hit the floor at which he stretched and started purring. I pulled back the curtains to find the rain had stopped and the sun had started to dissolve the mist over the field opposite. Perhaps life wasn't so bad after all.

Denzil followed me down the stairs with breakfast on his mind no doubt. I obliged and only then made myself a coffee. Tea had somewhat gone out of fashion in Well Cottage. Coffee and cider ruled and the proponent of the latter duly turned up at eleven o'clock or thereabouts. I decided that the hour was too early for cider whilst he did not. Thereby I was obliged to make a pot of tea after all because coffee was still a new fangled beverage to Old Sam. Denzil jumped up onto the dresser and sat upright keeping a weather eye on his old adversary.

Later Sam and I rather sloshed down through the orchard as the ground was so wet. I was carrying a pick-axe, one of the few useful tools I possessed. As we approached the well I noticed something that I hadn't seen before – a length of thick plastic hose, about nine inches long and sticking upright out of the ground at the edge of one of the two large slabs on the hedge side. I pointed this out to my companion in a matter that encouraged an explanation. Back went the greasy cap to enable a scratch of the forehead. "It be to pump water out. They'll have left it there for emergencies or summat."

That made sense to me. "You think it still works?"

"Most like. Can't see why not."

I could lever the slabs up without damaging the black pipe and I started on one straight away. I was making such heavy going of what should have been a simple task that I heard Sam wheezing and clicking in frustration. Sam could not contain himself to do other than gently take the pick from me and apply himself to the task in my stead. Despite his slight and elderly frame he manoeuvred himself into the right places and angles, the pick too, so that the first slab soon showed signs of movement. Working on the width of the slab rather than the length, the blunt side of the pick raised the concrete two inches. I bent down to place the fingers of both hand underneath in order to lift the slab upright.

"Stand back, stand back," shouted Sam with uncharacteristic authority. "You're cack-handed enough to fall right in."

I was not about to disagree and I move my hands right away sharply.

"There's a tump of timber in your shed. We could do with 'alf a dozen long-uns."

With the judicial use of the timber we edged up the slab safely in stages until it was standing upright on the edge of the hole the mouth of the well. Thereupon we laid it on the ground on its back as it were. In the half light I was somewhat surprised to see water glistening hardly six feet below the top edge.

"Water table's high," said Sam in answer to my unasked question. "All the rain what we've 'ad."

I grunted acceptance of his observation and bent to look closer. Should I tell Sam the purpose behind our work that morning? Tell him that I had intelligence that there could be a human body somewhere down that hole? I was thwarted in making a decision by Sam saying, "If you want to see if the water is fit for cider we needs a cup and a bit of string."

I obliged again and Sam lowered the cup into the water to draw it up slant-wise, the string being simply attached to its handle. I watched attentively as Sam took a sip, swirled the water round his mouth, turned, and spat the liquid out onto the grass behind. "It's tainted?" I exclaimed, expecting it to be so.

"Nope."

"No?"

"Sweet as a virgin's piss. Should make good cider."

I couldn't image what a virgin's urine would taste like and I would have lain a wager that Sam did not either. His drift seemed obvious enough."If one of your sheep had gotten into the well then that would have tainted the water, wouldn't it Sam?"

The old shepherd stood and thought a while. "Depends."

"On what." As the words left my mouth I had the answer in my brain.

"Ow long it 'ad been down there. The well would 'eal itself in time."

"How much time?"

"Depends. Months, a few years, maybe more."

Sam was insistent that we replaced the top slab back exactly as we had found it. "Don't want that cat of yours getting in. Ding dong bell and all that."

I agreed and we both laughed although mine was somewhat hollow.

By bedtime that day I had a strategy worked out. The first step was to repatriate the telephone – 'repatriation' meant to bring the darned thing back to Well Cottage and not to Normandy, France. No way was I going to be able to turn my face to the wall and try and kid myself that that I could ignore this third séance and get on with my life as though it had not happened. That was absolutely a no-brainer. I felt I could not ask Tom or Jasmine to deliver the telephone to me and so I had no alternative other than make a trip to London and collect the instrument in person. That decision having been made I experienced a welcome loss of tension.

Both Tom and Jasmine seemed delighted that they would have the opportunity to show off their new home to me – let alone the chance of divesting themselves of the miscreant telephone. Tom would be at home as he was most days and Jazz was quick to take two half days off work; Wednesday afternoon and Thursday morning. The die was cast and that was what happened. I took an early morning train from Hereford to Paddington, direct this time, and everything went accordingly to plan

I dared not ask what the price of their apartment had cost because it was absolutely sumptuous; a word that I have hardly ever used in a property connotation. The views both up and down the Thames were sensational even without the advantage of its spacious balcony. Two double bedrooms, both en suite, a huge lounge and a kitchen to die for – Jazz's words and mine – I marvelled at their achievement. I would have to admit to a nagging doubt as to the propriety of the money that had paid for such a luxurious home but – hey – who wants to be a party pooper?

I had to ask whether the telephone had rung on the Tuesday afternoon as expected. Tom confirmed that it had and the voice had not added anything to that which he had said before. Tom jokingly teased me that I had delayed my trip deliberately to avoid having to cope with the next scheduled miscreant call. I denied this – of course I did – but would have failed a lie testing detector machine.

The only other downside was a plastic carrier bag stowed temporarily close to the front door. They knew what was inside and I knew what it contained and the three of us fastidiously ignored the subject until it was time for me to depart back home. Talk about an elephant in the bag…

Back home I couldn't bring myself to place the telephone on the dresser in permanent full view. Nor in the lounge for similar reasons. Instead I popped the carrier bag on a shelf in the pantry. I was not expecting that it would burst into life until 2.15 pm the following Tuesday but should it do so, I would hear the ringing if I should be in the kitchen – where I spent most of my time when indoors.

The next part of my plan was to try and ascertain whether there was any evidence of the remains of a human body at the bottom of the well. If there were I had not a clue as to the stages of decomposition it might be in. In those days we did not have the benefit of search engines and efficient home computers and laptops .Nor did the Hereford library have such accoutrements as far as I was aware – at least the service was not offered to me when I turned up at their Help

Desk. Half of Friday I spent trolling through medical books and the like resulting in little enlightenment on the subject of the rates of human body decomposition when immersed in rainwater. What could I expect to find at the bottom of the well? Teeth took the longest time decomposing apparently, then thick bone, anything made of metal etc., even possibly parts of clothes.

During a leisurely lunch at the nearby Green Dragon I convinced myself that my next port of call should be the fire station. They would have any number of pumps capable of emptying the well in quick order. I walked across the Cathedral precincts into Castle Street, St. Ethelbert Street and thence to St. Owens Street. Three of the fire stations bays were shuttered whilst the other two were empty. On one side a large door led into an office where I found a lady clerk behind a counter in a room smelling of disinfectant and coal tar soap. Probably because visitors were a rare commodity ,she seemed quite pleased to see me.

I asked if the Fire Brigade offered a service of draining wells. I might have known that such a simple question would not necessarily have a correspondingly simple answer. She asked the reason as to why I required such a service. I could hardly tell her that an unconnected and decrepit French telephone had messaged my son to the effect that there could be the remains of a human body to be found in the well. She formally offered me a telephone number for Fire Brigade H.Q. but as an aside suggested that I would find the cost prohibitive. I would likely save considerably by approaching a commercial contractor. She was not allowed to offer names – the usual story.

Old Sam Williams would have to be my fallback position once again. I waited for him with a jug of cider at the ready and he, just when I needed him, was uncharacteristically late to the extent that I convinced myself that he was giving me a miss that day. But no, I was very pleased to hear the familiar tap on the kitchen door that preceded his stepping over my threshold.

"Evening Gaffer." He looked even more dishevelled than usual and his stoop was markedly worse.

"What's up Sam, you look as though you are carrying the troubles of the world on your shoulders?"

"Barney, one of my drinking pals down at the Dog and Duck. Been taken to 'ospital in an ambulance. Barney's missus reckons 'e's a gonner."

"What's he had – a heart attack?"

"Dunno. he turned yellow a while back – probably his liver, or kidneys. Sylvia's at the 'ospital now. There's no sign of 'er at 'ome. I expect she's there."

"How old is Barney?"

Sam chewed that one over whilst pouring himself a drink. "About seventy-six I reckon."

"He's had a good innings then," I observed perhaps too unfeelingly.

Sam glowered at me with both black eyes. "Poor bugger's 'ad a 'ard life, 'im and Sylvia both." I had the feeling that Sam was making a comparison between Barney's lot and my life of plenty.

"Oh, Sam, I'm sorry. Life is unfair as I know too well. Where has he been taken to, Hereford General?"

Sam nodded, "reckon so."

"Would you like me to drive you there? There may be a chance you could get to see him."

"That's kind of you Gaffer. The family will be round his bed. I'd be in the road."

"The offer's there. Tomorrow perhaps?"

"If I gets to see Sylva tomorrow I'll see 'ow the land lies."

A dewdrop appeared at the end of Sam's nose from liquid that had seeped though his black nostril hairs. Perhaps a substitute for a tear, I thought to myself. Sam pulled out a disgusting cotton men's handkerchief from out of his jacket and attended to the miscreant.

I topped up his glass feeling genuine sympathy for the old boy. "Can't life be a right shag sometimes?" That brought no reaction and I wondered if he fully understood what I had meant. Perhaps a change of subject was in order. "I'm thinking of draining the well to see what's lying in the bottom. Could do with a clean if we intend to use the water.?

"That's fucking daft," retorted Sam sharply. "Stirring up the sediment will make the water worse. Do no good at all."

I mentally was taken aback by Sam's reaction both with its aggression and use of bad language. I had hardly ever heard him swear before. "O.K. Sam, I'll level with you," I half lied. Sam had been present in my kitchen when the French telephone had rung for the first time last year and I remembered that he had made a quick exit, stage left. Whilst he had known that Peter was killed in France I had not made him privy to the details, nor those of Christine Palmer. I did not think that he needed to know or that he would have wanted to either. So I was not about to backtrack at this late stage and then have to explain the background to my genuine concerns about the well in the orchard.

"I've had a series of bad dreams, Sam. They centre on there being a body in the well. Somebody drowned in there, Not perhaps recently but since the well was constructed in the 1930s. So I want to explore the possibility of draining the well and putting my mind at rest."

Sam wheezed as he mentally chewed on this new line of information. "So that's what them questions about dead sheep was afore?" There was no question that he was suffering from advanced dementia or from ciderhead for that matter.

"Quite right Sam," I replied. "There's no flies on you is there?"

Sam almost smiled at the compliment. Back went his cap an inch or two to allow the obligatory scratching of his pate. "You means to drain the well?"

"I can't see any other way of putting the baby to bed."

"Putting the baby to bed?" he repeated slowly. "Aw, you means get the job done?"

"Yes, Sam," I agreed patiently. "I did think of getting the Fire Brigade to come out. They've got the right pumps for the job. I even went to the station in St. Owens Street."

"You didn't tell them what for, did yer?

"No, I made up a story."

"You don't want to tell them buggers nowt. Anyone what works for the Government. Don't know where it'll get you."

"No that was a dead end, Sam."

The old shepherd had another swallow to assist in the thought process. "If that there black pipe works alright the job'll be a good 'un."

"Black pipe?"

"Yeh – that pipe what sticks up outa the ground. What was used to draw water."

"Yes, of course." What a simple solution right there in front of my nose. "I'll have to lay my hands on a pump from somewhere."

"You'd be better off gettin' someone in what knows," rejoined Sam darkly, no admirer of my practical skills.

"You got any ideas on that score?"

Clicking, sniffing, a long slug of cider apparently supplied the inspiration. "Jack Taft over at Frostwick."

"How do I go about getting hold of him?"

Sam's eyes narrowed in that sly look of his when he gets into his sclemming mode; the same as I had seen when he found me the pig farmer that had robbed me over the bags of apples the year before. "I'll get word across to him if you likes?"

I hesitated. So Sam would make a few quid out of the deal. What did I care? "O.K. Sam, that would be very kind of you. But can we get the job done soon please?"

"I'll tell 'im that it's urgent."

That would mean that the price went up no doubt. As I saw Sam off some time later I repeated my offer to take him to the hospital to see his mate Barney, but I would swear that he was more interested in setting me up with his builder contact.

Sure enough, mid-morning the next day Sam turned up accompanied by a burly man, in his mid-fifties I would say, with greying curly hair, friendly sun-tanned face, stubble and eyes that missed little. He was obviously a builder judging by his dusty jeans and cement stained safety boots. If further proof were needed his hands were rough and puffy and his handshake strong. I offered tea or coffee but both were declined and we lost no time walking down through the garden and into the orchard.

Jack appraised the black pipe sticking out of the ground professionally as did he the slabs protecting the well, or rather, guarding anyone from falling in it. He made no attempt to lift one of them in order to observe the water level inside. "No point, we don't know how deep it is – not unless we get a piece of rope with a brick on the end."

I followed the logic. "So the game is to join a pump to the pipe and away we go?" I asked hopefully.

"And where's the water going to go?" asked Jack pointedly.

"Can't it just soak away in the orchard here?" I suggested.

"There'll be thousands of gallons down there, maybe tens of thousands," he added to greater effect. "Besides, it's been raining cats and dogs and the ground won't take no more; it's sodden now. Just look around. Are you on mains drainage here?"

I shook my head. "No."

"We can't get rid of the water that way then. What's the other side of this hedge?"

"A grass field."

"Give us a minute or two then." Over he went to the gate leading into the lane and disappeared. Sam and I stood around for a while trying to make idle conversation and after a while we walked a circuit of the orchard intent on examining the state and size of the forthcoming harvest and how I should seek to arrest the spreading menace of mistletoe. "Tenbury's Christmas Market is the place to sell mistletoe," offered Sam, "but you needs to take a right good tump to make it worthwhile."

Jack Taft did eventually come back whistling cheerfully and not a bit of an apology for leaving us for what seemed like half an hour. "There's a stream at the bottom of yon field," he said nodding in the direction of the perimeter hedge. "But we can run the pipe up through your gate and down the lane. Save asking the owner of the field for permission."

What I thought would be a straightforward and inexpensive job was growing like Topsy. "Can you give me a quote, please?" Parsimony, learned from childhood was kicking in.

Jack scratched his curly head as builders invariably do. "I reckon that I can do this meself." As an afterthought, "Sam could give me a hand." Sam could hardly contain his delight. "That'll save you a bob or two. But it depends how deep the well is and how long it'll take. Can't really give you a price right now."

I absolutely detested open ended pricing. I had learned from bitter experience that I would most likely get shafted. At the same time I could see the builder's point. "That'll have to do for now," I said quietly.

"I'll try and get over here Monday morning first thing. Are you free Sam?"

I hadn't noticed Jack's vehicle when he arrived that morning because he and Sam turned up at the kitchen door without me hearing them enter my front drive. My mood was not lightened as I watched the two men mount an almost brand new and large white, drop-sided lorry that said to me; "This bloke knows how to charge."

CHAPTER FIFTEEN

I would have liked to have given Sam the benefit of the doubt and ascribed his non appearance on that Saturday night to him being otherwise engaged in visiting his friend Barney at Hereford's hospital. My darker side suspected that he was either contrite at his subterfuge in his taking a backhander from builder Jack, or he wanted avoid giving me the opportunity of backing out of the deal in hand. Early on Monday he slid out of the cab of Jack's white truck like a cautious snake.

As soon as I was within earshot I asked about Barney. Sam stood stock still, removed his cap to chest level and with downcast eyes muttered, "He's passed over." This attempt at showing appropriate respect lasted hardly four seconds – much to my relief as Sam's bald pate was not a pretty sight at the best of times.

Jack threw down from the back of his truck several big rolls of blue plastic piping which the three of us carried down to the garden, into the orchard, and piled them close to the well. The sun was starting to dispel a morning mist and as the ground was reasonably dry Denzil decided to come down from the cottage to watch the fun. He was greatly miffed when I carried him back from whence he came and imprisoned him in the kitchen. No way did I want a pussy in the well to compound my difficulties.

Jack the builder commandeered Sam to help unwind the blue piping from out of the orchard and down the lane to the stream nearly a quarter of a mile distant. The two then ran an electricity cable from a power point in my garage to a fairly insignificant pump also rescued from the back of the pick-up. There were more shenanigans in trying to obtain a watertight connection between the pump and the black pipe sticking out of the ground to the side of the two heavy paving slabs. Believe it or not but builder Jack had not had the foresight to bring with him a range of different sized joining pieces. The pump easily joined to a short length of the blue pipe but the latter was a different diameter from the black pipe. Hence another hour was lost whilst Jack, ever cheerful, went off back to "his yard" to find the relevant remedy. Sam, the traitor, elected to go with him.

At long last the set-up was complete and the pump switched on. I thought that the appliance was working O.K. but what did I know about electric pumps? Jack fiddled about for quite a while before declaring that the fault lay in my black pipe. "It's fucking blocked solid," Jack announced in builders' language. "Not to worry he said, we'll have another go after I've had my bait. You putting the kettle on Des?"

'Bait', a Herefordshire word for docky or snap – a workman's lunch box – was a new one on me but I cottoned on in no time flat. I dished up Sam a rudimentary plate of cheese and pickled onions and left the two of them in the kitchen after making a lame excuse to go and sit in the lounge in order to sulk alone. At least, I would have been alone had not Denzil joined me lest Sam decided to throw his cap on the floor and show Jack his pick-up trick.

At least the sun was still shining as we re-assembled back at the well side prepared for the next round of the farce. Jack lifted one of the paving slabs ignoring most of the safety procedures that Sam had employed the week previously. He looked down into the semi circle exposed and I heard him distinctly mutter "Oh, shit". I queried his concern but was ignored. That did nothing towards relieving my angst.

A new, longer stretch of blue pipe was affixed to the pump and its other end dangled down into the well. I experience a wave of relief when Jack gave the thumbs up. He instructed rather than requested Sam to pop down to the stream and confirm that the water was being pumped therein satisfactorily. Sam had spent a lifetime receiving and acting on orders and slouched off to do Jack's bidding. I looked down into the hole expectantly for signs that the water level was dropping. Sure enough a band of wet bricks became slowly larger.

I decided to leave the two men and return to the cottage and get on with some chores – any chores would have sufficed to keep my mind occupied I reasoned. I was listening to an afternoon play on Radio 4 when Jack's curly head appeared round the kitchen door. "The pump's not man enough for the job," he announced without a hint of an apology. "I'll be back in the morning with a bigger one and I'll bring one of my lads with me."

I could have wept.

Sam thought better of turning up on the Tuesday and I was very glad that he did. The lad that Jack had promised was a gangly fellow, mid-thirties at a guess, and a face as dour as vinegar. I was soon to gather that his experience of travel outside the county boundaries was virtually non-existent, with one notable exception. His one passion in life, his only passion in life as far as I could ascertain, were the Baggies – West Bromwich Albion's Football Team. He visited all their home games and none of their away fixtures except if they played Aston Villa, Birmingham City or Wolves. Ask him any question about anything to do with the Baggies in about the last eighty seasons and almost invariably he knew the answer.

Even in my advanced years I never realised such people like Vince Tansy existed.

The more powerful pump was man enough for the job of lowering the water in the well and shortly before lunchtime that Tuesday Jack strolled into my kitchen and suggested that I follow him back down the garden. Vince was looking down into the well as we joined him. The second slab had been removed to allow more light to penetrate giving a gloomy view of the bottom some twenty feet or more down. The end of the pipe on the bottom was slithering like a wounded snake and trying to find more water in a muddy porridge. The pump was making the right noises to suggest it was devoid of any further conquest; job done at last. What a relief.

"Don't get too excited, Des," said Jack, switching the pump off. "Just watch down there." The half submerged end of the blue pipe on the well bottom started to disappear rapidly under a mixture that was obviously increasingly watery even at that distance. "It's filling up rapidly. The bottom's well below the water table and that is exceptionally high anyway 'cos of all the rain we've had."

I was catching on too quickly, my mind working overtime to search for solutions. "Couldn't you keep the pump running whilst the bottom is investigated?"

If we put a ladder down there, because of the depth, the angle of the ladder would mean that the bloke going down with have to jump the last six or eight feet on account of the angle – it would be too close to the wall for him to get right to the bottom. And if the pump failed for some reason, the rate that the water was percolating in, Vince could drown and I would be prosecuted by those Health and Safety bastards."

The way that Jack was talking I was under the impression that he was more worried about being prosecuted by the Health and Safety Inspectorate than he was in Vince drowning.

"Winching Vince down there would be a possibility but I worry about them well sides. Bricks are always dodgy and especially with gaps big enough to let water flow in at the rate that's flowing now. Don't forget that Vince would be on his hands and knees more'n like through the mud or whatever. If them sides collapsed I'm in trouble."

"Let alone Vince," I added.

"Yeh, him too. You could arrange to have the thing piled – half a dozen or so round the outside, inside if you get my meaning, but that would be specialist work and cost thousands and thousands – much more than the thousand or so you owe me. Besides I haven't got the equipment or skills to take that job on. You'd need a specialist firm for that one, Mr. Harper."

So now I was Mr. Harper and being softened up with an early warning as to what his bill might amount to. "The job's a bad 'un. An all round bad'un"

"We'd best get packed up and out of your hair. We all right for a cup of tea to have with our bait?"

Later I caught the builder driving out of my front gate. He stopped, lowered his window and grinned. "Of course, Des, if you're paying cash we could knock something off – and I won't then be charging you the V.A.T." That was the first time I had a glimpse of a smile on Vince's pallid face.

I was so wound up that I almost missed the 2.15 deadline that I had been dreading almost since I had last spoken to Jazz and Tom. I fetched the French phone from out of the pantry and dumped it on the kitchen table. Only reluctantly did I release the instrument from out of the carrier bag.

Slowly the minutes ticked by on the kitchen clock. Denzil was sitting upright on a chair washing himself whilst I paced anxiously in front of the Aga. I had recently had the cooker serviced, as soon there would be a need for it to operate permanently again. I had a hollow in my stomach exactly the same as I remembered waiting outside the headmaster's study in expectation of a caning – on more than one occasion. Despite my anticipation I visibly jumped at the sound of the first ring.

An amazing sight came to my eyes. Denzil had calmly been attending to his toilet yet on that first summons from the telephone he let out a king-sized yowl and fled in the direction of the lounge, the hair on his tail and lower back standing straight out at right angles. That did nothing for my nerves and I deliberately allowed for at least three more rings.

"Hello" I said into the mouthpiece almost as though I didn't know what the form was going to be.

"Help me, Help me."

"Where are you?"

"Help me. I'm drowning."

"Where are you?"

"I'm in the well, help me."

"Where is the well?"

"Help me, help me, I'm drowning."

There was more repetition and that was the sum total of the interchange. The telephone just went dead as it always had and probably the time the conversation lasted was much the same too. It seemed as though the spirits were given a set allocation which could not be exceeded.

I tried to analyse the whole scenario rationally. There was less intercommunication with the third spirit than the two previous contacts – in fact there was none. The spirit did not react to questions. Neither had Christine to any large degree. Only with Ricci had there been a definite two-way dialogue. However much I tried I could not tease out a reason for that. I was absolutely convinced that there was a body down a well somewhere or other. I was not too sure that was necessarily Well Cottage. In the daylight I would pooh-pooh that the call had anything to do with my home, but at night time I became increasingly unsure.

The big question emerged as to whether I could destroy the telephone and carry on living at the cottage and put out of my mind all thoughts that I might be sharing my home with a dead body and a restless soul. And if there was any substance to the claim that there was a body down the well, then up rose the questions "How did it get there? Was it by fair means or foul? Was there a possibility of another murderer to be sought out and be punished?"

One thing did cross my mind about the caller. Pilot Ricci had a definite American accent. Christine had hardly any. The latest caller, although I had very few different words to go on, sounded local – certainly to this part of Herefordshire. He sounded like any of the old boys who could be found in the Tap Bar of the Dog and Duck. That at least made the call and the situation more authentic.

There were practicalities to be taken into consideration such as how much money was I prepared to throw into an investigation. There could be any number of Jack Tafts waiting to fleece me. O.K., I wasn't exactly on the poverty line but who deliberately throws good money after bad?

I was disturbed in my pondering by a telephone ringing. Not the single rings favoured by the French but the joined up kind here at home. "Hello Dad." Jazz not Tom; I had obviously been promoted to "Dad" status. Had they secretly gotten married? "How did it go?" she asked.

"Are you speaking from the flat?"

"Yes, I've taken the afternoon off work. I am so interested to know what's happening."

I told her the bare bones and went on to explain my misgivings and lack of positivity as to what the way forward might be. She came up with a couple of off the cuff ideas before realising that doing so was not the way forward. We agreed that we would both think on and talk further.

Denzil followed me back into the kitchen and jumped onto my lap at the first opportunity. I wasn't sure that he was seeking to give me comfort or find some of his own. I settled for 'probably a little of both'. I seriously debated throwing the dratted telephone down the well in the orchard and seeking out a suitable estate agent in Hereford to market the sale of Well Cottage. I was in theory as free as a bird and able to relocate to anywhere I chose. Instead I eventually put the instrument back into its carrier bag, opened the cellar door, and heaved it inside. I heard it hit the floor below with a satisfying muffled, mechanic thud. "Take that you bastard thing."

Jazz did get in touch that night and I was still "Dad". She sounded excited. "I've had an idea. The police use divers to go down wells."

"I can hardly go to the police, Jazz. They would need good cause to send a diver down and the chances of them believing my story will be zilch. They'd write me off as some sort of nutter."

"I agree wholehearted," replied the girl earnestly, "but you could hire a diver privately."

"Oh yeh, do you know how many miles Hereford is from the sea?" I retorted with undisguised sarcasm.

"They have diving clubs inland," replied Jazz patiently. "They practise in lakes and things – plenty of those in Wales. Besides,' have diver will travel', as the saying sort of goes. You're not all that far from the sea."

"I think that idea's cock-eyed," I said, giving it no credence.

"Leave it with me. I'll do some research."

I had no doubts at all that she would.

Tuesday went into Wednesday and Wednesday into Thursday, Friday and Saturday. I was missing Tom, of that there was no doubt. Although I saw little of him when he was beavering away in his office upstairs, just hearing his telephone ringing and his pacing the floor and coming into the kitchen for a rare coffee break was comforting. The unconscious knowing that he was about the house I had not quantified at the time. Perhaps I needed to move out and get back into the mainstream of life again.

On Saturday the telephone summoned me and my immediate thought was Jazz would be on the other end. No such luck. "Is it to be cash?" said Taft cheekily. He gave me the two prices and expected me to choose; with or without an invoice? As there was such a sufficient difference I metaphorically sent my apologies to the VAT officials, then H.M. Customs & Excise, and agreed to have the booty available for Jack to collect "come Tuesday" in his words. If anyone from H.M. Revenue & Customs, the successor Department to the C & E is reading this now, may I remind you of the Statute of Limitations – i.e. out of time?

Shortly after Jack Taft, I was pleased to hear from Jasmine. "I have found the Knighton Sub-Aqua Club and they're based in Knighton as the name suggests. That's not too far away from you Dad, is it? Anyway a guy named Harle has heard me out and told me, in his words, he will 'gladly listen to our requirements'. He sounds very genuine and a bit of an anorak too. He says that he will ring you tomorrow lest you are at church. I told him there wasn't much chance of that."

"Clever girl," I thought and said.

I entertained Sam as usual that early evening, even though I was still annoyed with him for sucking up to Jack the builder and profiting at my expense in the process. For all his rough ways, the old sclemmer was sensitive to atmospheres and he ploughed a cautious course in handling the situation. For want of much to say of an amiable nature I told him of my new plans that would lead to an examination of the bottom of the well and his services would not be required..

Sam he tried to suppress an involuntary curling of his top lip in exchange for a conciliatory smile and I found the process quite amusing. He did not tell me I was completely bonkers but I knew he would have liked to. Our conversation almost immediately returned to the safe subject of discussing the forthcoming apple harvest and how we might find a replacement for Peter.

I relied on my house telephone at Well Cottage. I did own a mobile but the cottage was in a blind spot reception-wise and so when I gave a contact number to people it was invariable my land line. Yet just down in the village, at the Dog and Duck for example, there was a signal as I had witnessed when there with Peter.

The extension next to my bed rang at eight o'clock that Sunday morning. That was unheard of. In those few seconds before I groggily lifted the handset I imagine all manner of worrying scenarios. "Hello, Mr. Harper?"

"Yes."

"It's Harley."

"Who?"

"Harle from the Knighton Sub-Aqua Club. Didn't your daughter tell you that I would contact you?"

"Ah," my brain found the correct gear. "Yes she did, but not at," I strained to see the clock, "at eight fifteen on a Sunday morning."

"Oh, is that all it is? Sorry. You have a problem with a well so I am told?"

"Yes, I do, I want the bottom examining ."

"And the well's full of water?

"Yes, that's correct."

"I'm sure that we can get over that problem, Mr. Harper. I need to come and see for myself and weigh up what needs to be done. Would later this morning be O.K.? Say about eleven o'clock?"

I was pleased to agree and gave the caller directions to my cottage.

Denzil seemed suitably surprised to see me up so early on a Sunday morning. I wondered how much cats could differentiate between the days of the week. If every seventh day their breakfast bowl was at least an hour later would that register in their brains? The reception Denzil gave me that morning would support the theory.

I made myself a coffee with single cream, my favourite, and a bowl of cereal. I had tried sharing my cream with Denzil some months back but he refused my generosity point blank. I wondered what the origins were of the saying "the cat that got the cream".

CHAPTER SIXTEEN

From the lounge widow I saw a largish Bedford van pull in uncertainly into my drive from off the lane. Not until I opened the front door did I get full vision. White may have been the underlying colour but the bottom half of the vehicle was caked in mud with streaks travelling to the topsides and even to the roof as well. Only the windscreen was clean and perhaps only so in order to display two names flamboyantly displayed across the top; HARLE on the driver's side and NAT in the other. Wasn't that a trend of the 1960's?

From HARLE out popped a young man, about twenty-five at a guess, wearing a pinkish-red vest, tattered blue jeans that looked as if they had been washed a thousand times, and with a heavy pair of bright yellow work-boots on his feet. His exposed arms were completely covered in a medley of coloured tattoos that stopped just short of his chin and which promised that his whole body would be a similar work of art. Yet the most significant first impression was he owned one of those facial expressions that promised cheerfulness, honesty, and fun. The young man rushed round the van intent on shaking me by the hand.

NAT took her time in alighting as if she wanted to make her own splash once the ripples from her companion had somewhat abated. Slipping out of the passenger side I noticed at once that she sported body art as well but hers, what I could see anyway on her arms, was sparse and selectively placed. Long brown hair, swept tight back into a pony tail, blue hoops on white for a sleeveless top, clean pink slacks and white trainers, she would have passed for a sixties chick any day of the week.

I knew I could relate to these two even before a word was spoken.

"Harle is Harley I suppose? I said pleasantly, meeting his outstretched hand with mine. Nodding at the artwork that engulfed his exposed flesh I added, "And I do I draw the conclusion that your Dad was a biker?"

The young man laughed spontaneously, "You're bang in the nail there, Mr. Harper."

"Call me Des," I said loud enough for the girl to hear.

"I think that my mother was to blame for the Harley handle. My father favoured Lancelot."

"Was he into King Arthur and his knights?" I jibed.

Before he could reply Nat advanced and without warning unbalanced me by planting a dainty peck on my left cheek. "Natalie, pleased to meet you."

I ushered them into the cottage and through to the kitchen. I had half expected Denzil to fall in love at first sight with pretty Natalie and I was not to be disappointed. His tail went straight up as he wove himself excitedly round and in between her legs, begging no doubt to be picked up and petted.

"Coffee?"

"Please," said Harle.

"Would it be possible if I had milk?" asked Nat.

The visitors seated themselves and Denzil seized the opportunity to jump onto the girl's lap.

"What a tart," I said to her.

"She's lovely," she replied..

"She's a he called Denzil. Biscuit anyone?"

Eventually I got to explain the nature of the job that I was hoping for them to be able to carry out. All I kept back was that I was half expecting to find human bones in the debris at the bottom of the well. I related Jack Taft's concerns about the well sides caving in and stressed that there was no way I wanted anyone to take risks. I did not say that I had in the very back of my mind a serious concern that the voice from the telephone could be leading people into a trap – just as had the supposed voice of Pilot Ricci.

"I can see the builder's point," conceded Harle. "But diving should be safer on that score providing that the brickwork is basically sound. The weight of the volume of water in the shaft should keep the brickwork in place unless I start hacking away at it. I've done a couple of wells before – one of them for the police wanting to retrieve stolen property. You'd be surprised as to what gets thrown down wells."

"So you are fully qualified for this type of work, Harle?" I asked.

"Sure am," he replied nonchalantly.

Natalie piped in with a whole string of acronyms for qualifications I had never heard of. "You have no worries on that score, Des."

An unexpected wave of guilt passed over me to the extent that I felt I should come clean about the possibility of Harle finding human remains. A flash of inspiration came to my rescue. "There's an old wife's tale I heard in the village, that there's a body down there. I would like to put my mind at rest by proving there is no truth in it."

"Ho, ho," Harle laughed. "Your daughter told me the search was for a gold wrist watch."

I felt my face colouring. "I honestly didn't know that. She was using her initiative I suppose. She's a bright girl. Not my daughter actually – my son's girlfriend. Lucky fellow. She presumably told you that porky lest you refused to have anything to do with the job. Does it? I mean, will you still do the job?"

"I take it that the water's not tainted? Your builder would have sussed that out?"

"No, it's not. I'm positive."

We walked across the garden, into the orchard and down to the corner and the well. Denzil tried hard to slip out of the kitchen and join the party and was imprisoned in the cottage for his pains again. Both visitors admired the myriads of apples adorning the trees and were knowledgeable enough to recognise them as good for cider making only. Natalie made the point clear to me that cider was her preferred tipple. I took the hint and promised her some of the golden liquor come the New Year. Under my breath I added "should we ever get to make some."

Harle made short work of lifting one of the heavy paving slabs, tattooed biceps straining. What it was to be young and so fit, I envied. "How deep is the well?"

"Twenty odd feet, the builder said."

"No problem. I will need to get the van close by."

"The gate yonder leads into the lane and the ground has firmed up after that rain," I indicated.

"Right, we just need to fix up a convenient day for you Des. I expect you will want to be here when I go down?"

"Of course, if only to provide you with refreshments."

"Shall we say this coming Thursday?" Harle looked across to Natalie to get confirmation from her as well as from me.

We agreed they would turn up next Thursday at ten o'clock or thereabouts. They were thereabouts sort of people confirmed by neither of them sporting a wrist watch. I did think about asking the price but chickened out. I did not want to be seen to be churlish.

The next day's priority was to nip into Hereford to visit my bank and draw out the cash I would need for robber Taft. I took the opportunity to purchase four kegs of draught cider with a mind to give one to Natalie later in the week, given a successful outcome to the investigation of the well.

On the spur of the moment I visited a huge out of town caravan dealership. Before I found a salesman, or more pertinent, a salesman clocked me, I walked round the hundred or more second hand vans displayed in the outside sales lot. Some of the prices I found staggering, especially the motorised homes. Luckily, I thought, I found several which appeared to be the same model as Tom's and so I made a mental note of their details.

Still no sign of a sales person, I retraced my steps and entered the doors leading into a huge showroom, stuffed with new models and with an extensive spare parts counter set to one side. At last I was identified as a potential customer and a middle-aged man, smelling of an overpowering aftershave, approached me with that all too apparent fixed smile associated with salespersons. Apart from his perfumery, he quite reminded me of poor Peter.

I used the numbers from the models I had noted in the lot outside and said that my son had a similar caravan less than a year old. Having established I was not a buyer but a seller the man was not impressed by my attempt at a pitch. "There can be a wide divergence in price between models designated the same number. Did your son buy the van from us?"

I didn't know. I really didn't know. When asked, I gave Tom's name and my address. The man went away and returned pretty quickly. "Yes, your son Tom did buy the van from us. It wasn't new but not very old either. If he wishes now to sell the van we would be pleased to make him an offer."

"Can you give me some ideas as to what that offer might be, please?"

Mr. Smelly had obviously anticipated my question – or that was the impression I received. "No, sir, we would need to see the van."

"A ball park figure?"

"No, sir. Sorry, sir."

Jack Taft knocked my door just after eight o'clock that Tuesday morning – obviously his first port of call for the day and on his way to his first job, judging by the two lads sharing the cab of his pick-up truck – neither of whom I recognised. Come to that I did not recognise the vehicle either; another nearly new model. He had caught me in bed literally with my trousers down and I perceived a whiff of impatience on his part when I eventually opened the front door. He wanted to take and count the money on the doorstep but I insisted that he did so on the kitchen table.

In total contrast to the two visitors of the previous day, Harle and Nat, Denzil's non-welcome was a raised tail deliberately to show the button of his anus as he walked away. I thought to myself, "That cat's a weather vane for sorting out the nice guys from the bad. I must pay more attention to him in the future."

Taft's attitude changed to one of joviality as he stuffed the notes, duly counted, into a back pocket and offered me his services at any time I should need them in the future. With arses on the brain I would dearly have like to tell the man to stuff any ideas of future involvement up his. Instead, like a lamb, I showed him out of the front door.

As soon as the hands on the kitchen clock touched two fifteen my mind was never far away from the cellar floor underneath. The French telephone was, I imagined, still lying on the cellar floor as it had landed when I had tossed it from the top of the steps. Perhaps it was so damaged to be incapable of ringing? On the other hand the instrument had never possessed the mechanical or electrical capability of ringing. To solve that conundrum I was almost relieved to creep up to the cellar door and lend my ear to its woodwork as the hands on the clock slipped towards the quarter. "Ring… Ring…" My question was answered. Needless to say I walked away and out into the garden sunlight.

On Thursday I was not immediately aware of Harve and Nat's arrival as they drove straight into the orchard from the lane and were fairly advanced in their unpacking when I joined them. Harve was struggling into a wet suit and I glimpsed his chest, as expected, a jumble of body art. Meanwhile Nat was reading dials on a pair of oxygen cylinders. Both the paving slabs had been lifted and set aside exposing the circular mouth of the well. I looked down inside and reckoned that the water level was restored to "normal" which was lower than it had been during the last exercise as there had been hardly any rain in the last week or more.

Nat was wearing the same sort of outfit as before although the hoops on her top were of a different colour. She obviously favoured the sixties look. I watched as she hammered two long iron stakes in the ground a yard or so away from the well's edge. I took their orders for beverages but waited, curious to see the purpose the stakes served. From the van Nat collect a roll of something that soon revealed itself to be a Jacob's ladder. One end was attached to the stakes and the other she unrolled down into the well to become submerged in the water. I was alarmed at thinking the ladder would not reach the bottom, but stopped myself pointing this out to the girl by realising that there was enough for Harvey to float up to and secure his escape. On that note I retired to the kitchen to put the kettle on.

Denzil seemed to know that his adored Natalie was within his curtilage and he gave me no end of abuse because I had interfered with his cat flap to make it inoperative. "I'm doing it for you own good," I explained in vain.

Milk for Natalie and a small coffee for Harle. "Piddling in a wet suit is not to be advised," he had grinned. For myself a mug of tea.

Natalie went to lift an obviously heavy generator onto the ground from the back of the van. "Let me do that?" I offered.

"It's very heavy Des," she said, "best I do the lifting." Pretty well effortlessly she accomplished the task. A little while afterwards I thought to test the weight of the machine and grabbed both handles as I had observed Nat do. Blimey, I really had a struggle to get the thing an inch off the ground. I am sure that Natalie watched me out of the corner of her eye.

The generator, I learned, was to provide power for a light for Harle in preference to a torch, as well as a vacuum pump that could suck up disturbed sediment and allow Harle clear vision. The latter necessitated a pipe up and out of the well to drain away in the grass some distance away. Apart from the power line to the torch there was another to allow Harle to converse with Natalie and a third for reasons I forgot to enquire. All in all quite a palaver.

At last, generator noisily throbbing, two oxygen cylinders strapped to his back, rubberised hood with large oval face mask, the diver confidently swung his bare feet into the well, a booty bag and trowel in hand, and descended the rope ladder, jumping the last couple of feet into the water and disappearing from sight.

By this time Nat was wearing earphones and a microphone combination which kept her in touch with the diver. She was able and willing to give me a running commentary. It was as slow as a cricket match with a couple of stonewallers at the crease. All there was to see were bubbles in the well and a brownish liquid escaping onto the orchard floor. After about half an hour Nat announced, "He's coming up".

Harle's head appeared almost before the words were out of Nat's mouth. He struggled up the rope ladder until his head came level with the rim and he was able to divest himself of the bulging bag by throwing it over the rim onto the grass. From there he popped out of the well with athletic ease. I disciplined myself not to turn out the contents of the bag but instead offered a warm drink which was gratefully received. Harle's bare feet were showing signs of their exposure to the water and Nat was already off in search of a towel.

Later we turned the bag out onto that same towel and raked though the contents. There was lots of rusty stuff, some obviously parts of a bucket, many unidentifiable bits and pieces and a few coins, too corroded to immediately reveal their dates. Certainly nothing of a human nature. "And that's it," concluded the erstwhile diver. "I plumbed the bottom of the well. The floor is made of bricks lain on their side – no mortar so as to be pervious along the joints."

I left the pair to allow Harle the privacy of changing out of his rubber suit whilst Nat started the process of cleaning their gear and loading their van. This took more time that the unpacking and setting up. Of course I offered lunch but they had brought with them sandwiches and some sweet items for energy, as well as a thermos. Mid-afternoon the pair were ready for the road. Time for me to pay for their service.

The amount Natalie ask for astounded me – I was almost lost for words except for "I'm not having that." Judiciously I had drawn sufficient money from the bank the day before not only to pay Jack Taft but also in anticipation of settling with the diving team as well. I went in search of my wallet in the cottage and drew out an amount I thought fit. Back at the van I caused not far short of a row because I wanted to pay them nearly three times more than they had asked for. I won in the end by threatening all manner of ramifications if they continued to refuse. And when I handed Nat the keg of draft cider…

I went to bed that night certain of the fact that I had made two new friends. What price the sense of relief knowing that there was not, and probably never had been, a body in Well Cottage's well.

CHAPTER SEVENTEEN

Jasmine contacted me on the Friday night. I had expected to hear from her the day before, soon after the diving team had finished their investigation. She mumbled some excuse for the delay which I failed to hear properly

"So, did they find some evidence of a body, Dad?"

"Nothing whatsoever and I am absolutely certain that there is nothing of the sort down the well. If there had ever been a drowning or whatever, then the body must have been removed. The diver did a very thorough job."

I could almost hear Jazz's brain ticking over; probably speeding in overdrive. "How can you be certain of that?"

"Because Harley, the diver, described the brick lined bottom to me. He is a real genuine guy. He brought up a bag of debris, everything just about that wasn't sediment, and we all picked through it. There was nothing."

"O.K., if you say so," said Jazz, somewhat dubiously I thought."Why should this third voice be a false alarm when the two others definitely were not?" I felt that she was asking the question of herself rather than to me particularly. "There must be something we're missing."

"No, Jazz," I almost yelled down the phone. "This is the end of the line – it's driving me fucking nuts." I rudely cut her off.

My conscience kicked in and so within the hour I rang Jazz back in order to apologise. "That's alright, Dad," she said sweetly,

"I can understand how uptight you are. That's quite acceptable for a man of your advanced years." Her cheekiness banished any tension that was left in me and we laughed together."By the way, what is the age of the well in the orchard?"

"Sam reckons it was dug out in the 1930's."

"1930's – how strange."

"Why's that strange?" I asked not at all expecting the bombshell she was about to drop.

"When was the cottage built Des?"

"I dunno exactly – early nineteenth century I suppose."

"And has it always been called Well Cottage do you know?"

The shell exploded. "No, I don't know," I replied slowly. "There could be another well, is that what you're getting at?"

"Worth investigating don't you think?"

My heart was again close to the bottom of my stomach. Jazz had a point of course – I was quick to see that. I was loath to say it outright though. I contented myself with a diversion. "At least I can get a sledge hammer to that French phone and throw the bits into the well we do know about."

"No, no, don't do that, please Des. Not until we have a total resolution – one that we can be sure about. Look, Tom and I were discussing taking a drive on Sunday and treating you to Sunday lunch. We could bring the phone back with us, see you and kill two birds with one stone. How do you feel about that idea?"

"Killing birds is one thing but this problem is killing me. I just want rid of the whole thing."

"I know you do," said Jazz soothingly. "And you will soon. Once we have confirmed that there isn't another well at the cottage I promise you, on my life, that Tom and I will personally throw the dratted telephone off Tower Bridge and into the Thames." For greater effect she added, "Right in the middle."

I weighed up sticking to my guns on the one hand or relenting and having the pleasure of Sunday lunch with the two people whom I loved most in the world (Denzil not qualifying as a person). "Sunday then, what time shall I expect you?"

"About noon. I'll kick Tom out of bed and no Sunday papers."

Lucky for me but unlucky for Tom. "Shall I book a table somewhere?"

"No Dad, our treat and our venue. We can all squeeze into my Golf."

In the year that I had known Sam I felt that I knew his quirks pretty well. He turned up Saturday evening for his couple of "harns" of cider (or three or four more like) and I asked him a question. In truth many of my questions he viewed with a suspicion brought about by his lowly station in life but he seemed exceptionally guarded when I asked, "Do think there's another well somewhere about this place?"

" 'ow do you mean?"

"How long has Well Cottage been called Well Cottage?" I said, putting the question in the simplest of terms.

Up went the hand under the peak of his cap for the classic scratch of the forehead. Somehow there was something slightly contrived about the action on this occasion. "I wouldn't know, Gaffer," was the disappointing reply. "Tis Barney's funeral on Monday." Surely an awkward attempt to change the subject? I let the subject drop as I had a better source in mind.

I might have guessed that Tom and Jazz would not settle for less than the most sprauncy dining venue in the whole of Herefordshire; a country house in the Golden Valley. I would have loved roast beef and Yorkshire pudding but instead had to wrestle with French cuisine the likes of most of which I had never heard of. On the other hand my two hosts were apparently completely at home and pleased to render translations for my benefit. Our bottle of red wine cost more than half a case of average Bordeaux at my local vintners and I felt relieved that I was not expected to pick up the tab when the time came.

Inevitably the conversation touched on the French telephone and what its fate should be. Much against my better judgement I agreed to allow Jazz to take the instrument back to London under the terms of a promise that it would be despatched into the Thames when I so decided. I warned Jazz our future friendship depended on her keeping her word. Her green eyes met mine reassuring me that the agreement was sealed.

Back at the cottage I sat stoically in the kitchen as Jazz descended into the cellar and retrieved the carrier bag with the offending article still inside. She and Tom examined the telephone in the hall, pronounced that there seemed to be no serious damage. I insisted the thing should be deposited in the boot of the Golf and not remain under my roof for a second more than necessary.

"The cellar's empty," observed Jazz when back in my kitchen.

"We did have cider stored down there in the cool in the spring and summer. Sam has an aversion to going down there and after this, so might I."

"It's a useful space," observed the girl. "Although I did detect a certain sort of – well – atmosphere."

"Probably too damp for use as storage," I suggested.

"In London that would be have been tanked out and converted to living quarters."

"But this isn't London, Jazz – thank goodness."

"Yes, thank goodness," Jasmine agreed. "I couldn't live out here in the wilds for all the dresses in my boutique."

'For all the tea in China' had been usurped. Such is life.

I waved them away with a prayer that I had seen the very last of the French telephone and my life would return to the rural idyll that had attracted me to this corner of Herefordshire. Yet I still had one burning question to resolve. When had Well Cottage first been called by that name?

Monday morning I drove into Hereford to find the County Records Office which was situated in an unlikely quarter of the city. My sense of purpose was thwarted by a notice on the door announcing it was closed on Mondays. As I came back through the village I saw a hearse standing in the road and a coffin, Barney's I assumed, being carried by four bearers through St. Edmunds lytch gate. Sam would no doubt be sitting amongst the congregation. Would there be a wake in the Dog and Duck later in the day? As I only had known Barney by sight I would not be expected to attend.

On Tuesday I followed the familiar path into Hereford, entered the Records Office and found myself in front of the necessary counter. I expected to find a spinster lady, perhaps with tortoise shell glasses, hair in a bun and wearing thick stockings. Or, maybe a bowed, wizened man sporting a grey beard. Instead I was greeted by a cheerful young girl with a smile that revealed she was pleased to receive a customer who wasn't there for the purpose of genealogy. For that reason perhaps, she threw herself at the task of satisfying my query. Out came a plethora of old maps from what I recognised as from a large, flat set of drawers similar to those used by architects. Together we could not find any reference to when my cottage was built but a parish map dated 1888 caused my spirits to drop. My cottage was annotated "Well Cottage".

"By no stretch of the imagination could my cottage be given that name for any other reason other than…"

"Hardly likely," the pretty archivist agreed. "We haven't discovered the date when your cottage was built but I would imagine that it was the site of the first well in the village. It does not necessarily mean that the well was, or is, in the cottage's curtilage. It might have been close by – yours being the nearest dwelling."

A glimmer of hope? I was not convinced however.

Jazz phoned that evening. "I left Tom in charge of the Frenchie this afternoon as I was at work. The thing performed as usual; just a one way dialogue and nothing extra said. Tom tried to tell him the well was empty – the voice just talked over him. It's so frustrating."

I recounted the results of my visit to the Records Office. "It certainly looks as though there was a connection with an actual well at least since 1888 and possibly much earlier."

"What about searching out a local historian, Des? You might be surprised at the depth of their knowledge. Isn't it worth a try?"

I chewed the idea over long after I had broken contact with Jasmine. Perhaps there was some sense in that. How would I find such a person?

Next day I walked into the village and entered the local shop. Thankfully the proprietor was serving at the till rather one of his part-time women. He was of the old school and always insisted on calling me "Mr. Harper." I put my quest to him and the answer came straight back at me. "The Reverent Walsh, up at the vicarage." And rather cynically, "He's got too much time on his hands. Always delving into local history, he is."

The vicarage was very obviously set beside the church and was a structure to be admired for its architecture. A woman in a housecoat answered the door to my summons. I knew the vicar to be a bachelor and a strong advocate for gay marriage and, if village gossip were to be believed, a proclivity in that direction himself. I felt therefore, safe in assuming that the lady standing at the half open doorway was fulfilling a housekeeping role and nothing more intimate.

"Any chance of a word with the Reverend?" I smiled.

"Church business?" she asked, obviously assessing me as to which box I would fall into.

"I want to tap into his local knowledge," I said. "I live up the road in Well Cottage."

"Oh, right," she said opening the door further. "You should find Ian in the churchyard. He's trying to decipher one of the oldest gravestones. If you go between those two trees," she nodded to the hedge line to the right, "you'll find a short cut."

Sure enough I found something like the old boy who had eluded me behind the counter in the Records Office; an aged man sporting a white goatee beard but still exhibiting vestiges of athletism. "Reverend Walsh?"

The man straightened up trying hard to contain a grimace of annoyance at having been disturbed. "Quite so."

I introduced myself as Desmond Harper, owner of Well Cottage, in a tone of voice that I had once used in formal situations in the City of London.

The vicar quickly decided that here was somebody who was not about to be fobbed off – and might even be some sort of nuisance if not a danger. He turned on his practised benign ecclesiastical smile and his mind from the far more interesting weather washed letters on the gravestone. "What can I do for you Mr. Harper?"

"I am hoping to tap into your knowledge as a local historian, please?"

Now that did cheer up the Reverend Archibald Herbert Walsh. Gravestone forgotten, the vicar reverted to his smile of pleasure. "We could talk in the vestry if you prefer?"

"No, I'm quite happy out here, thank you. It's a pleasant morning."

"What would you like help with?"

"I live in Well Cottage in the lane up yonder. Do you know anything of its history – especially as to how it got its name? There is a well in the orchard but I am told it was formed in the 1930's."

"I didn't know about that one," frowned the vicar. "Well Cottage has a long history."

"I traced the cottage back to 1888, in the Herefordshire Records Office," I said trying to impress with my investigative work.

"1888" laughed the vicar. "The cottage, or at least its name, goes a long way further back than that. Your cottage was built about 1820 but the one before that earned its name from the well there."

"Oh, really?"

"People were building wells and similar in the Neolithic era, many thousands of years BC – before Christ. Yours is a relative youngster; probably fifteenth or sixteenth century. There was no piped water in those days so wells assumed great importance. Not just for human survival but for domestic animals. So a well in the countryside was of importance, especially a public well."

"Was mine one of those?"

"I can't answer that. There seems to be no surviving record that would testify to that. But yours was not the first dwelling on the site and I know yours owes its name to a predecessor; the name has been carried on."

"You don't happen to know where the original well is, or was?"

"No. They were often located in the kitchen or cellar or outside, close to the house."

"Why was there a need for a second well in the thirties?"

"No idea," replied the churchman quickly. "Any number of reasons."

"Could be the original well dried up or became tainted do you think?"

"That's possible. Could be there was a change in the water table, that's not unheard of, or that the water lost its sweetness."

"And then it would have been filled in?"

"Your guess is as good as mine. I wouldn't rule out it still being there. What's the construction of your kitchen floor?"

"Limestone type flags; originals I would say."

"Could be a well under them. Is the cellar the same?" I nodded. "Then there's another possibility. People in the olden days tended to be frugal by necessity and filling in wells tended to fly in the face of their attitudes at the time." The man picked up the disappointment on countenance. "I'm sorry I can't be more specific Mr. er Harper, did you say?" And then he added trying to be helpful, "You might engage the services of a water diviner and his dowsing rod."

"Would he be able to discover a well under stone flags?"

"I don't honestly know. Worth having a word do you think? There's even a chance that one of the pensioners in the village might remember the well. Old people's memories of their childhood can be remarkably accurate."

"Can you give me a name I could start with, one of your congregation perhaps?"

The parson thought hard and I could see that he was genuinely trying. "Margaret Bliss might be worth a try. She grew up your end of the village and lived here all of her life until she was obliged to move into a home. She can't walk but there's nothing wrong with her brain. I visit her quite regularly."

Soon after I took my leave and wished the vicar luck with the interpretation of his chosen gravestone. "I'll have my very own soon," he retorted with alacrity.

I was on a roller coaster and there was no chance of getting off. Next port of call would have to be the Three Elms Home for the Elderly in Canon Pyon. The elm trees had long ago succumbed to Dutch Elm Disease. Although I called without a prior appointment the manager welcomed me and whisked me upstairs to a room at the end of a long corridor. I was to wait outside whilst she checked that Margaret was in a fit state to receive a visitor. At no time did she warn me as to the state of Margaret's comprehension. I came back out after just fifteen minutes of having been bombarded with requests for pear drops, Fry's peppermint creams and Rowntree's fruit pastilles. I wondered if the Rev. Walsh had deliberately set me up.

Feeling stymied as to where to go from there the idea of approaching Elizabeth Palmer came into my head. She and her family had lived in Well Cottage after all and my street credibility with her was assured. I telephoned that afternoon.

After the necessary pleasantries Liz responded to my question confidently. "The original well is in the cellar Des. You will find a circular stone with an iron ring set into it. We never had it up all the time we lived in the cottage so I don't know what sort of state it's in. Is there anything else you want to know?"

"No Elizabeth. Thank you so much for just spoiling my day," I said with humour.

CHAPTER EIGHTEEN

I delayed my descent into the cellar for as long as I could before the shouting in my ear of "coward, coward" reached fever pitch. That equated to Friday afternoon. Denzil watched me open the cellar door and resolutely sat on his haunches safe in the kitchen. There seemed a justice of sorts in a coward like me having an equally cowardly cat.

The light down there was a sixty watt bulb; enough for the dispensing of cider but too poor for any detailed work. I walked back into the kitchen and through to the pantry where I picked up a hundred watt bulb. From the dresser drawer I brought out my torch, grabbed a tea towel, then descended the stairs into the cellar with a contrived sense of purpose. I stood under the light intent on changing bulbs. I switched on the torch; nothing. Not even a faint dying glow. I made a mental note to buy replacement batteries – there were none to be had in the cottage.

I took the new bulb from out of its paper sleeve and then deposited it where I could handily retrieve it from my jacket pocket. Wrapping the tea tower round the lighted bulb so as to avoid burning my hands I pushed up and twisted to release the bulb from the socket. Dropping the towel and bulb on the floor I search for the new bulb in the darkness. I shut my eyes tight during this manoeuvre as somehow that made me feel safer. Happily I twisted the new bulb home at the first attempt and bright light flooded the cellar.

The stale air in the cellar was a given, considering the lack of ventilation but the earthy smell from damp seeping through the walls was too reminiscent of a coffin in its grave for my liking. Initially I had not been too concerned about my cottage's cellar. Perhaps some of Sam's distaste had worn off on me. Certainly, over time, I had become to hate the underground cavity more and more.

I knew about the iron ring set in the floor which Sam had passed off as a means of securing animals for slaughter. That may have been a guess or a deliberate falsehood. My money was on the likelihood the ring served as a means of raising the lid covering the well I had been searching for. First I needed to remove the hessian that covered the whole of the cellar's floor. This proved surprisingly easily as, old as it was, the fabric remained largely intact as I rolled it carpet-wise up against the far wall.

What was exposed was another carpet of ancient dust, perhaps the accumulation of half a century and more. I decided that I ought to sweep that into a corner and retraced my steps back up into the body of my cottage and the sweet air of the kitchen. Denzil watched me with cat's curiosity as I exited by the back door and returned with a soft broom.

I was obliged to wear the tea towel as if I were a highwayman such was the cloud of dust created by the most careful manipulation of the brush. At one stage I had to retreat back up top in order to escape the assault on my lungs. Denzil's tail bushed in alarm at the dust covered and masked interloper. That was a pleasing note of humour.

Allowing time for the dust to settle I returned to the cellar with a pail of water which I sprinkled all round the floor. Although creating a thin mud that stained the ancient flagstones the end result was much more easily achieved.

I could see then that the ring was inset in a circular stone about thirty inches in diameter. From the gunge that filled the crack around the edges of the circle I reckoned that the lid had not been raised in many a year. How many? Tens of years perhaps. If there were a body in the well then it should be no more than bones and unlikely to be too obnoxious. Then again, there was no saying that the well hadn't been filled in some time in its past. Perhaps when the new well in the orchard was commissioned?

If only for that possibility I was reluctant to call in Harle and Natalie on what could turn out to be a complete wild goose chase. On the other hand I knew that the laid back pair would take such an event in their stride. No, I would need to take a gander inside the well before deciding the next plan of action.

There was nothing for it other than to make my way to the bathroom, strip and enjoy a warm, cleansing shower. At least Denzil was quick to recognise me for who I was.

That evening I could see as plain as a pikestaff that Sam wished that he had never shuffled though my kitchen door. The cause of his dismay? – I had put it to him that he came and helped me open up the well that following morning. He argued that was a job better suited to Jack Taft and his boys who had all the tools and means necessary. I lied "That may be my reserve position but I would like to try first myself, or ourselves."

"We'd need special tools Gaffer."

"I've thought of that," I countered. "We need a long and substantial iron bar and I have one of those in the garage." I had inherited the bar which was stowed in the rafters in the garage. I often wondered what its use might be and now I had possibly found the answer.

I could not resist an attack. "You knew all the time that the well was under that iron ring, didn't you?"

Sam's face told me he was searching for the words that would make a lie more believable. He failed. "Perhaps it crossed my mind," he said with exaggerated precision.

Sam's appetite for cider that early evening was uncharacteristically muted. When he left I was not at all sure that he would put in an appearance the following morning.

For a change I rang Jasmine that evening rather than her ringing me. I brought her up to date with recent events. She said that she was impressed with the fortitude I had demonstrated and made me promise to give her a blow by blow account of future developments. I agreed and made her confirm that the destruction of the French telephone would be carried out the moment the cellar 's well had been explored and no body parts found. Even so, despite her agreement, I didn't know whether I completely believed her.

If I had had even an inkling of what a momentous day Saturday would be I would not have left the snugness of my duvet.

Sam slouched in to the kitchen bang on ten o'clock as we had agreed. He examined the metal pole that I had rescued from the garage earlier and tried hard to find fault. I had not noticed whilst it was lying on top of the rafters there was a fifteen degree bend about eighteen inches from one end which made me believe that I had discovered its actual purpose. I carried it down the steps into the cellar with Sam grumbling close behind. He looked about him failing to comment on the results of my cleaning efforts. He had only eyes for the iron ring in the floor; almost a fatal fascination.

I threaded the smaller length of the pole through the iron ring as far as the bend. This short end finished just before the rim of the circular lid. I pushed up the other end and had the satisfaction that I had created a viable lever – hence confirming in my mind as to the iron bar's original purpose. I applied more pressure and the near edge of the stone lid resisted at first and then, as I broke the seal of accumulated dirt, lifted a few inches. That was enough for the moment. With Sam's help I needed to work out a plan of action.

There were several possibilities as to how we could lift the stone lid up and manoeuvre it clear of the entrance it was designed to protect. Sam favoured levering the stone high enough to place a wedge underneath before pushing the lid higher. The lid was heavy but lighter than I expected. By levering the lid as far as the iron bar would allow and employing my set of step ladders to keep the long end of lever static. We could then take one side each and bring the lid to an upright position. With Sam pulling and me pushing we could roll the lid out of the edge of the hole. Rolling, like moving a barrel on its side, was far the easiest way to handle such a heavy object.

Sam demurred to my idea ungraciously, his eyes smouldering with discontent. He declared that he would go get the step ladders and some wood only because he did not want to be left in the cellar alone if I were to go and find them. I might have expected him to be laggardly; anything to delay descending back into the bowels, but I really thought that he had nipped off back to his home he was so long.

Just before I was about to abandon my station and go in search I heard him wheezing down the stairs. I set the step ladders in what I judged to be the best strategic position and slotted the iron bar into position. Sam decided to help with the lift and up came the heavy lid. The exercise worked so well that instead of stopping to push the timber under the stone as an interim holding point, we pushed our end of the bar right up and secured the end on the platform at the top of the step ladders. That allowed both Sam and I to be hands free.

The idea then was for us each to grab a side of the lid opposite each other at its widest point, then pull it upright when it would stand virtually on its own. What happened next would haunt me for the remainder of my life.

We had the lid almost upright when Sam issued a cry of anguish. He lost his footing and slithered feet first into the exposed mouth of the well. His loss of grip on the stone caused all its weight to accrue to my side and it was too heavy for me to hold. Down fell the lid and settle snugly in the whole to where it belonged. If Sam were conscious and shouting down in the body of the well no way could I hear him.

I froze petrified. I don't know how long for; probably only seconds. Nightmare was too soft a word. Incredulous? – definitely. My god, what the fuck do I do now? I grabbed the iron bar from off the floor, my shaking hands fumbling to re-insert the end into the iron ring and find the original position necessary for leverage. This achieved I threw the whole of my weigh onto the bar in the attempt to raise the stone lid. Nothing happened other than to bruise my stomach. I was to learn later that the lid had dropped back into a slightly different position and had consequently jammed – the fit not being perfect.

Sam might have been treading water, shouting up at me with all his might and I could not have heard a thing. Nothing that I did had the slightest impression on the stone lid at my feet. The only possible remedy that came into my head was to tear up the cellar stairs and ring 999. The operator was frustratingly cool, as she was trained to be of course, before she determined that I needed an ambulance and the fire brigade. I rushed back down the cellar and shouted at the impassive stone hoping that Sam might be encouraged knowing that rescue was at hand. I took up the iron bar and tried relentlessly to shift the stone lid.

Of course, one disadvantage of living in the back of beyond is the isolation from emergency services. After what seemed an eternity I heard the approach of a siren and rushed out of the cellar to be on hand to give directions. Can you imagine my distress when I saw a white and orange police car overshooting my front gate. "Not the fucking police – what fucking use are they going to be? And who asked for them anyway?"

The driver, obviously realising that he had overshot his target, came reversing back at a reduced rate of knots and swung into my drive in a splash of gravel. The officer on the passenger side had the door open. "My man's in the well," was all I could think to say not realising that fact had already been relayed to them. I led the way, as fast as I dared, down into the cellar. The driver followed soon after and I begged them to join me in putting our combined weight on the iron rod. Even then the stone would not budge. The driver suggested we bounced on the rod rather than a steady pressure and at last the stone moved upwards. The three of us managed to lift the round stone right away and roll it into a corner of the cellar.

"Got a torch?" one policeman demanded.

"Not here," I replied.

The other policeman ran to their car and came back with a yellow monster. We all crowded round the hole. There was a glint of water some twenty feet below and what looked like a circular plate; Sam's disgusting cap.

"Looks like he's a goner," observed the driver almost laconically.

"'Fraid so," agreed his mate.

I near enough burst into tears, desperate to take the weight off my trembling legs lest I fell over.

A second approaching siren distracted my attention and with a new sense of purpose I went up to meet a red fire tender.

Six large firemen in yellow helmets bailed out and followed each other into my cottage. It could have been a scene from the Keystone Cops had it not been so tragic.

A single medic turned up soon afterwards in a saloon car painted gaudily in large green and white stripes. He explained that he was the fast response unit and apologised for arriving in third place. I led him down to join the congregation in the cellar. I listened to the ensuing confab between the nine would-be rescuers feeling totally detached from the proceedings.

Their unanimous conclusion was that whoever was in the well, if indeed there was someone down there, would be long dead. "No point in anyone going down there," they all agreed. "Job for the police diving unit." They would need to be called out from their base in Birmingham.

Policeman No.2 turned to me. "We need to go upstairs, Sir, and I'll take some details."

Sitting in my kitchen across the table from P.C. Wayne Daly, it started to dawn on me that I could be in some serious trouble. I wasn't given a police caution at that stage but just about everything I said was fastidiously recorded in the officer's notebook. The interview lasted a good half hour in which time the other services departed and the police drivers made diagrams and measurements of the cellar and recorded its minimal contents. Before they departed the police sealed the cellar door and instructed me not to go inside under any circumstances until the diving team arrived.

They turned up within the hour closely followed by a detective sergeant and D.C. Withers at his elbow. She recognised me at once and made that clear to her companion by openly informing her superior that my son Tom was on licence from an Open Prison. D.S. Cornish led the ensuing interview and was worrying thorough. I fell into the trap of lying about the root cause about why I had put in train the opening of the well. I could not bring myself to relate the story of the French telephone and the totally improbable events that the instrument had led me into. My evasiveness must have affected my body language – something that the police were particularly trained to pick-up and act upon.

One of the diving team interrupted us and whispered in Cornish's ear, loud enough for both Withers and I to hear, that a body had been found in the well. That was the cue for me to be taken to Hereford Police Station in the back of their car. I made an excuse that I needed to secure Denzil in the lounge during my absence. The poor cat had sought refuge under the dresser in the kitchen through the whole sad episode. He was no doubt overcome with all the comings and goings. I filled up his bowl and imprisoned that in the lounge with him just in case my trip to Hereford should be a protracted one. I didn't give a thought to him needing to do his rear-end business.

In retrospect I might have been glad that I was out of the way whilst Sam's body was winched up and carried out to what I imagined to be a black mortician's van.

At the police station I was given what I would describe as a pretty stiff interview. Still I had not been cautioned nor invited to make a written statement. Nevertheless I was uncomfortable before, during and afterwards and grateful to be offered a lift home with a couple of traffic officers who made a detour on my behalf in the course of their normal duties.

Denzil was pleased to see me and be released from his temporary confinement. I headed for the whisky bottle and poured myself a treble; especially needed when I saw a notice on the cellar door forbidding entry.

Sufficiently fortified to be confident of not breaking down I telephoned Jasmine and Tom. Both, in turn, were astounded and then appalled at my news. The conversation was a short one.

I was pretty well in my cups by the time I hit my bed that night and as a consequence I slept fitfully, batting off the whole plethora of images that had filled that Saturday. To make matters worse my bedroom was invaded by flashes of lightening and long rumbles of thunder. I imagined that Sam was letting me know how disgusted he was with me. That thought was really unnerving.

I did have lucid moments towards morning when I tried to analyse the best plan of action to counter the police investigation which was pretty well bound to follow. My ultimate fallback position, the one of last resort, had to be to recount the whole story of the French telephone and just hope I could somehow make it believable. I would need to inform Jasmine and get the instrument into my safe custody. Little did I know then I had been the unwitting architect of my own misfortune.

CHAPTER NINETEEN

As I attended to Denzil's needs that Sunday morning he could be forgiven as to wondering why I was so desultory in my greeting. He expected by right to be Top Cat and that morning he certainly wasn't.

Jasmine waited until what she thought was a safe hour before ringing me. "I've been thinking Des…"

"I have done nothing but think these last twenty-four hours," I moaned.

"Yes, yes, we're both so sorry for what you've been through. I wish I could come and give you a hug. Tom is just as concerned as I am. Poor Sam and poor you."

"Go on Jazz, what have you come up with now?" I said rather brusquely to counter my rising emotion.

"Are you ready for this?"

"Anything. Nothing could be worse."

"I think that the last voice on the telephone, the third voice, was Sam's." said Jazz coolly.

"You what?" I exploded.

"The first two spirits were involved with historic events and to a limited extent we could interface with them, to ask questions of sorts. The last voice was different. There was no interaction at all and we both agreed the caller had an accent local to you. The body in the well wasn't in the past but in the future this time. That's what I think anyway."

Images of Ouija séances flashed into my head. Of me and Angela in our old house with the plate rail round the walls of the dining room and my suspicions that the spirits, mischievous if not downright evil, ended up sitting on the rail once their messages had been delivered. The concept that these were similar spirits making contact through the French telephone was one that I could embrace even if no other person could. That explanation would fit all.

"You could well be right, Jazz – the evil spirit lured Sam to his death. Is that what you're saying?"

"Something like that," she replied.

"How can I sell such a story to the police? I may be under suspicion of having deliberately caused Sam's death."

"They think that you might have pushed him in?"

I told the girl about my interview at Hereford Police Station the previous afternoon and that it appeared that my file was very much open.

"Surely not?"

"I'm not kidding. It's no laughing matter. As the last resort I am going to have to tell them the whole story. At least I would pass a lie detector test with flying colours. And I might have another pesky voice on the telephone that they will be able to listen to. That should do it."

"Oh no," said Jazz with a huge sigh.

"What?"

"I don't know how to say this, Des," the anxiety in her voice ringing out. "I haven't got the phone anymore."

"You what," I strangled the words..

"You've been urging me to get rid."

"It's in the Thames?"

"It should have been, Des."

"Should have been?" My voice had involuntarily climbed a couple of octaves.

"Only yesterday I decided that you deserved peace of mind and I would go along with your wishes. Whilst Tom was doing his business here in our apartment I took a local train into Waterloo, then the Tube to Tower Hill. It's only a short walk from there to Tower Bridge. I had the phone in a carrier bag intending to throw the bag and all into the river."

"I feel a 'but' coming?"

"I was sitting on a District Line train with the carrier bag on the seat beside me. There were some lads in the same carriage, about seven or eight of them. They started fooling around and as I was intent on watching them. I think that one of their number stole the bag. Thinking about the event afterwards I am pretty certain that my attention was deliberately distracted."

"Bloody, bloody hell."

"At the time I though "good riddance", they'd saved me a job and, with luck, brought trouble for themselves. Although I expect they've sold the phone on by now. What an irony that we may still need the damned thing."

"I don't suppose there's any point in trying the Underground's lost property – just in case it was taken by mistake?"

"We could try if you like Des. I'll do that right now."

Jazz was as good as her word. The telephone had not been handed in so far but a kindly employee had suggested that not all lost property was handed in at once. She took contact details from Jazz but, over time, nothing came of it.

I was charged with the murder of Samuel Arthur Williams shortly afterwards and remanded in HMP Hewell, near Redditch, for fucking four months until my trial at Worcester Crown Court. Hewell was a multi-category prison and I found myself banged up with some very distasteful characters. Those were the worst days of my life barring the death of my darling Angela. My solicitor reckoned that I had been refused bail because I was seen to be the head of a criminal family. I had Tom to thank for that.

I did not tell my defence team about the French telephone as I feared that I could end up as a mental case in Rampton Secure Hospital or somewhere similar. My trial was very much touch and go according to my barrister and happily I was acquitted on a majority verdict. I believe I had to thank Harle and Natalie as much as anyone or anything else. Their credibility and testimony, so honestly given, demonstrated to the jury that as I had searched one well thoroughly, it was believable that I had good reason to extend the search to the other. The Reverend Walsh, my local vicar, also helped my case.

The apple harvest that season was a non event as regards cider making; the fruit lay rotting on the ground where it fell. If Sam was in Heaven watching, something I do not believe, then he would be shedding a tear or two for the golden stuff that would never see the insides of a "harn or two".

As soon as I was incarcerated in Hewell, Jasmine took Denzil to live with her and Tom in their apartment in Putney. The feline traitor seemed more than happy to exchange a master for a mistress and a garden and orchard for a warm flat with panoramic views over the River Thames and London Town. Jazz wrote of him sitting statuesque at their lounge window or, as the days become warmer, on the balcony, surveying the world below as if he were king.

I came to see this for myself as I have stayed with Jazz and Tom on several occasions since my acquittal. Denzil always gives me a warm welcome, rubbing his sleek Felix marked body against my legs and singing a series of meows. He knows when I am about to leave because when sees me packing my suitcase that is his signal to make himself scarce lest I try to take him away with me. One cool cat who knows where he is best off.

Even if I had wanted to I would not have repatriated the devious moggy. Tom loved him but Jasmine adored him, as he did her. It would have been cruel of me to have insisted on my rights of ownership.

I did return to Well Cottage when I regained my freedom but there were too many ghosts to cope with; Sam of course, Christine Palmer, Peter and, Denzil too. In due course I sold up and moved far away.

Where to? I'm not telling.

I still get nightmares about Sam Williams. I keep imaging that sordid greasy cap of his floating motionless on the black water down the bottom of the well.